i write,
HE DICTATES
-A love story

i write, HE DICTATES -A love story

Arnold Iwin Francis

PARTRIDGE
A Penguin Random House Company

Copyright © 2014 by Arnold Iwin Francis.

ISBN: Hardcover 978-1-4828-2036-2
Softcover 978-1-4828-2035-5
Ebook 978-1-4828-2034-8

All rights reserved. No part of this book may be used or reproduced by any means, graphic, electronic, or mechanical, including photocopying, recording, taping or by any information storage retrieval system without the written permission of the publisher except in the case of brief quotations embodied in critical articles and reviews.

Because of the dynamic nature of the Internet, any web addresses or links contained in this book may have changed since publication and may no longer be valid. The views expressed in this work are solely those of the author and do not necessarily reflect the views of the publisher, and the publisher hereby disclaims any responsibility for them.

To order additional copies of this book, contact
Partridge India
000 800 10062 62
www.partridgepublishing.com/india
orders.india@partridgepublishing.com

Preface

Arnold is just extra-ordinary where writing is concerned and after reading the book you'll talk in the same tongue as I do now. After reading so many books and novels I find no one can come even close to my husband's writing—judge for yourself.

Mrs. Pamela Francis

I have read a lot of authors and I'm just fascinated by them but the way 'i write, HE DICTATES-A love story' is written gets me intoxicated for the words are like diamonds studded on platinum on sheaves of gold.

The alphabets squirm to get into articulate magic words that cascades on the ear-drums like a lucid, melodious tune. No one who loves to read and appreciate would want to get out of its realm.

Mr. Praveen Subarna & Mrs Candy Subarna

My Dad has got a hand that cultivates a harvest of words even on a sandy soil.

Now that the book (i write, HE DICTATES-A love story) is published I feel GOD must be really dictating to my dad for writing such a master-piece.

Ms. Freny Cherry Francis & Mrs. Seema Francis

Hoodwinking a Policeman

The Hard, sprawling year 1945 lay soft against the feet that had been trudging for long hours much against its own wish.

The feet looked Indian in a foreign land—two brown ones amongst the thousand white ones—the country was Hitler's Germany.

In a country besot with Nazis such an incredible incidence would invariably be taken with a pinch of salt, but my dear readers who have turned into my friends take it as gospel truth from someone who shirks lies like the plague and the one who narrated this episode, most likely, was a very truthful person.

The policeman waved to the cyclist to stop—he did, "why is the light on your bicycle not on?" the policeman thundered in his gruff voice. Pat came the answer "because the dynamo on the cycle works only at high speed". "Come on, show how it works?" the policeman retorted. The cyclist jumped on to his cycle and took off like lightning while the policeman looked gaping at the receding figure till it was out of sight—soon the two wheels were in the safety of its home and what a sigh of relief for the man.

Never Lose Hope

This also happened around the same time maybe a difference of one or two years.

Some medical students bunked their classes to go for a dance just outside the periphery of Germany—to be precise it was Luxembourg.

These boys carried no passports, Visas or Identity cards to enter this country. But boys are boys and who thinks of such trivial things when itinerary was just to clasp a girl on the wooden floors.

The sentry on duty guarding the entry and exit point of Luxembourg was approached who with a stern look and "care too hoots attitude" made the boys shudder. The icy look froze the wooden floor and the idea of the dance melted away in the cold only to spew venom on this God-forsaken soldier in silence.

Long lingering minutes passed, misery writ large on their faces, their drooping eyes would have burst like a dam had they not been boys and tears would have made furrows on their clean shaven faces smelling of after-shave as though they had a fight with the bottle.

In despair, all four looked at each others' faces hoping an angel of mercy would wave his wand to dispel this as a dream. But what faces them was a steel-like reality and there was no way except to return to their faithful hard beds.

Who said miracles don't happen—they did around 1945.

The hard-piercing eyes of the sentry penetrated deep into the folds of the heart of the boys, smirched everywhere was girls and more girls. He thought of his own girl, his wife and the 16 year old daughter he had. His heart missed a beat and the hard coconut cover took on the hue of the white of the inside. A soundless whistle and a blood-red finger of his brought the boys running to him.

They could cross over to Luxembourg, hold the girls to their heart's content but like Cinderella would have to return at the stroke of 12 of the clock for there would be a change of guard.

The boys' prayers had been heard. The more vociferous, an atheist amongst them had even defied God and said loudly for all to hear "if there is a God why doesn't He help them cross over to Luxembourg without any hurdle". The others had silently beseeched God in their prayers to grant them this wish and they would never again commit any mistakes that did not savour in God's favour.

Gingerly they stepped onto Luxembourg and sank into it as though it was a Persian carpet and unrolling (the carpet) would bring the 'Cleopatra' of their choice.

The half-hour drive to the dancing venue was an unabated silence though each chest heaved to its enormity to splurge out words that never saw the day of light for the tongue sprayed 'sweet nothings' in silence for their mouths were sealed in excitement.

The wheels purred to a halt but in the presence of the crescendo of silence, the thud of the brakes sounded like the trumpet of an elephant, nay, nay it was the roar of an enraged lion of Africa.

Eight eager eyes narrowed to a slit to absorb 'their dream come true', eight ears spread out their antennae to catch the slightest strum of guitars emanating from the wooden floors of the dance-hall like a bat her sonar, their nostrils dilating to merge their after-shave with the "Night in Paris" that the girls wore thick on their frocks.

The cab driver's directions were thrown to the wind which cooled the haughtiness of it and swept it into the folds of the sky to come down later as snow.

Their feet of lead froze them to the ground but their desire to meet the girls glided them to the dancing hall.

"Garden of Eden" of Biblical fame could not have been sprayed with so many adjectives, with a purr "beau-ti-ful", "heaven on earth", "Mind boggling", I can't believe it "am I dreaming" all gurgled through the velvety tunnels of the boys' throats. What they saw they could not perceive. The Silhouettes of the men and women gliding on the dance floor to the soft lilting music that ever so softly hit their ear drums got them intoxicated. Was it the flow of music or the rhythm of music of the couples on the wooden floor? Who was to tell?

The four stood petrified and chilled to the bone. Were they statues shivering in their own pants? Would they gather the courage like honeybees invading other people's garden to gather nectar and pollen from the lovely red roses? The bees had stings to ward off an enemy but didn't they have the disarming smile which would melt any girl in their arms like iron in a 1500 degrees Centigrade furnace. What if the girls refused outright or were discouraged by their mothers not to talk to strangers.

They were so close and yet so far from the reality of their dreams. Their destination had arrived but were they like the dog that had chased the bone so long and had got dog-tired that he could not enjoy the succulent bone. The boys whisked passed all their anxiety, all their fears.

The feet of lead dragged the over anxious torsos of the boys while the heads kept reminding them to be cool. How they wished they had cucumbers to cool them. The air was cool much cooler than what Indians would ever prefer and yet scalding hot lava from the volcanoes of their heads erupted and their inner vests were drenched with perspiration.

With clenched fists, one of the boys bowed in front of the beauty in ivory, a "Venus" come alive and asked her for a dance. The smile on her face showed him she was all too eager for she had sat without a partner for long-there were more of the fragile fairer sex then there were the rough, muscular boys.

When his clenched, clammy fist opened and when her fiery fingers slipped into the palms of his hand it was a dream of a lifetime come true.

The others though hesitant did not miss the cue and were on their toes. Their knees swept the floor as they poured their sweetness asking the lasses for a dance. The too eager white hands turned crimson at the touch of the masculine, rough, bison-skin hands of the boys. Both manoeuvred each other round and round the dance floor as though it was a needle in a gramophone on a long playing record. Time stood still and all wished the clocks would never tick again. The clocks did tick as they always do oblivious of the desire of the boys. The hall gyrating to the rhythm of music, the guitar strings were in a frenzy as they heaved up and down with the frequencies the guitarist strummed. The drums could not be restrained from keeping in sync with the lead-guitarist whose fingers moved with precision and electrifyingly.

As the music moved to a crescendo, so did the pairs whose legs moved like one—their faces were close, their noses almost touching each other, the nostrils belching out the carbon dioxide which sat happily on the sweet-nothings poured out by the boys and girls to each other. One furtive look at the gorgeous frocks which billowed like an umbrella in a storm showed the trousers straining to come closer and closer to the owners of the six piece frocks. Both were lost in each other and I wonder if they knew of their own existence. If there was heaven on earth, certainly this was the place. It was writ large on their faces. The old ladies sitting on the far end, exchanging glances with each other could be heard through their whispers for they were on their favourite subject, gossip.

Love was blind so they say and so do I but the couples on the floor were unabashed or, all that mattered was the rhythm of the movement of their synchronised feet, should not miss a beat of the music-it didn't.

The shiver that runs down the spine and through the whole body at the touch of human bodies of opposite poles was uncontrollable. The pulse rate ran alarmingly high to a crescendo and not the normal 72 beats per minute and any quack doctor would have suggested an I.C.U. (I see you, you don't see me meaning a heart attack and death.)

The electrifying sensation that strikes like lightning at the mere touch of the fingers lingers on as though chocolate was in the mouth and we don't wish it's sweetness to melt away and recede.

The guitar strings kept their rhythmic vibrations fluctuating with every beat of the number breathing life into every couple as they whisked past the drummers round and round the wooden dance floor.

On top of the music the M.C. rode whispering "rest-a-while" much to the annoyance of the younger generation and a breather for the oldies. All could be seen scampering to their seats, the boys very gallantly leading the girls to their places. Some requesting the girls to keep the next dance for them, some politely and gingerly asking the newly found girlfriends if they would care to come to the cafeteria for a coffee or a drink. Many would oblige, others would hesitatingly take a retreat with a profuse "no thank you".

Everything in this universe has a magnetic attraction, the high and the low tides on the seas being the pull of the moon, the guitarist from strumming the strings of his guitar, the M.C. couldn't stay away from his microphone sending waves of invitation in his deep throated voice of 30 hertz to the couples to take to the wooden dance floor.

There was a flurry of boys rushing out to the seated girls requesting them if they could have the honour of having the next dance with them.

It was a slow fox trot and the boys could be seen pulling the girls closer to them and most girls would willingly yield to the temptation. The entwined fingers would tighten their hold like that of the soldiers, would in precision keep in step. The ambience of the place was like Srinagar's Sharvan garden only no flowers bloomed here but a different species of every hue in myriad colours blossomed in the form of a bud—Eve beguiled by the serpent and Adam trespassing where the Lord had forbidden him.

When your arms are circling a beauty's waist which foolish boy would waste his time on his fore-fathers like Adam and Eve. He is so engrossed in holding the white, fragile hand that such thoughts do not even come in the periphery of the halo of his brains.

The M.C. himself was oblivious that he was solely in-charge of the "going ons" in the hall for he was dancing away with his girlfriend. Time stood still as far as they were concerned till an usherer came to remind him if the elderly didn't need to rest their feet.

The couples did find it difficult to separate for many were engaged in very serious conversation that would change their course of life and only love birds would understand such dialogues. Away went the girls to their respective seats with some of the boys still in toe. If only they could manoeuvre their talk and make the girls willing partners, would they tow their life boats into seductive waters and make a nest, bursting with the feathers of love and whose tendrils would leave a nostalgia for both of them to dip the fingers in and shudder with the very thought of this heavenly bliss. Boys to the bar and girls to pamper their faces with another touch of rouge in the washroom.

The girls were busy pushing and pulling their 'unmentionables' and on their favourite subject 'boys' couldn't stop their tongues from wagging.

Their kissable mouths making all the designs and patterns that this planet earth could have ever witnessed, from a lovely "o" to the shape of the crescent of the moon, to the tongue lolling out of the captivity of the mouth with phrases like "oh! He's a he-man with such a suave tongue; he's all muscles, oh! He's such a gentleman". The M.C. could be heard clearing his throat over the microphone which multiplied the volume of his voice manifold so that every remote corner of the hall would reverberate and a wry smile on every face would be evident. The deep throated voice of the M.C. had taken over and it was a waltz that the couples had been invited to. They were not a very happy lot except for the old fogies who seemed to have let their hair down and were thoroughly enjoying every move with their old, wrinkled partners. It was more to show their prowess at dancing for they slithered like a snake in perfect unison. They had over the years mastered the art of keeping their ladies close to the heart even if it was a waltz number, much to the chagrin of the younger couples.

Most of the couples had a change of partners and were busy introducing themselves to each other. Some had found the girls they held, from the same colleges they studied in; some from adjoining towns but all were busy making the most of it and didn't let any opportunity slip by.

So you hail from Munich and before she could answer he asked her what she said her name was? You didn't ask for my name and I didn't tell you. In the din of the music you could hardly hear anything and it was more of a Chinese whisper, a game where you whisper something and the one next to you hears something else. All you do is almost push your ear into her mouth to hear and if she refuses to talk and prefers to nibble your ear you are at her mercy.

When coffee brews the aroma of it spreads like wild fire and everybody takes deep breath with their nostrils dilating to the maximum to unknowingly pilfer the free abundance of its flavour in the air-love also seemed to be brewing in small quarters in the dancing hall as it does in every corner of the world, some places kindle with fury others only for procreation of children. How else do you see the population explosion? If you put your thinking caps on, when the world is inebriated with love where does the word "war" even find a place in the dictionary, leave alone in our lives. Solitary confinement shows we can't live without each other but then world wars and hatred manifests itself.

Turn our gaze and back we are on the dancing inseparables. Promises are being made some to be carried to eternity, others will vanish as dawn erodes to dusk, day after day night after night. Some girls who wouldn't let their partners subdue them keep a face right through the dance as though butter wouldn't melt in their mouths; they want to be independent and yet don't want to miss out on the fun. They are impervious to the chocolate melting words and are like the rain falling on the windshield of the car to be wiped away by the wiper. The seven colours of the rainbow adorning the sugar coated words, making a fringe like wisps of the girl's curls falling on the ivory skin of a beautiful face, were just like alphabets fitting into the wrong slots for her making no sense.

Boys and girls had started pairing. Girls who had been out on their first date saw the first pair of trousers and fell for the guy even if he carried a crooked nose and his eyes were perched at a slant and his ears resembled that of a bat. He was the most handsome boy in their eyes and no amount of persuasion would ever change that view. How else would love be blind? They open their eyes only after marriage and perceive through the dermis and the epidermis the real him. Besides the crooked heart, Hell's fury couldn't be churning out a more scheming wife.

Amidst all these was a couple who felt their pulse beats alarmingly high at the mere touch of her long, nimble fingers in the sturdy palms of the boy's hands but actually gingerly held on to the tips of her fragile fingers or so they seemed.

NEIL, as he spat out his name in her ears and that he had come to study in Germany all the way from India had a magical effect on the girl. A girl as demure as her, hearing he was from India found something in common. She also hailed from India, from Lahore to be precise.

What happened next no one seems to know but all hell broke loose. A girl who had quietly been holding hands and dancing had all the questions piled up on her tongue. Only a psychologist could be called in to answer such queries as to why such a sudden change of behaviour when you see your own country-men whom you have never set eyes on earlier. "Atta-boy, so you also come from India? Which part of India"? And before Neil could answer "Delhi" she was on to the next. "What are you doing in Luxembourg?" "No, no, not Luxembourg but Germany that he was studying in". "So you are going to become an engineer, mechanical, chemical or electrical." "No, no, I'm studying medicine and will become a doctor." "Promise, you'll treat me free when I'm sick." "Okay, okay, I promise you I'll treat you free." The dance carried on at its pace but she was oblivious of the many feet and faces that came and passed her in the dance hall on the wooden floor. The more she talked the more he wanted to hold her tighter. She was becoming irresistible and he felt he was drooling at the mouth like a baby. Was infatuation turning into love at first sight or was it love for his own country, India and its people, especially for this hitherto coy, soft padded in the right places, a girl who wagged and wagged her tail, no sorry, tale with her tongue which refused to stay in a closed mouth for want of fresh talk like blood gloats for oxygen of the air.

My myriad readers, young and old, who have sailed in this boat of love will discern, not in dismay, how palatable love is and how gullible and incorrigible you become once you set your foot on it.

Neil was holding five manicured delicate fingers as though he had found, right in the middle of the wooden dancing hall, a treasure whose hands smelt profusely of 'Night in Paris' fragrance. It looked she had a bout with the scent bottle. Some of it had even splurged on to his own hands as he squeezed her hands in his till she squealed 'not so tight'. The beautiful six-piece frock she wore fluttered with every move she made. He felt he was in the hands of a Goddess and he wanted to just smother her in his muscular grip to leave the shadow of his imprint on her.

The M.C. had already blown the whistle like a foot-ball referee with 'rest a while' and all inseparables had separated and strutting to their seats except for these two who were still gliding to what tune no one seems to know. They would have continued had not peals of laughter greeted the antennae of their ears. Embarrassed they retrieved her place and both sat down-love flowing like Ripples of water over stones and pebbles in a stream.

The cup of hot coffee that Neil and his friends relished at such times was a thing of the past, for the present and future were holding his hands and he hers, a bit tighter than she could bear. Her lovely pink hands had been deprived of colour, for the red hue of the blood had stopped flowing but every pore oozed out love.

Mother's love, father's love, brother's love, sister's love had all deserted in front of the huge waves of this tsunami and all that even dared slightly were swept off their feet and drowned in this catastrophe of love for this tantalizing beauty. When confronted with a woman's love, all other loves go for a walk. Imagine a total stranger coming into your life and becoming a part and parcel of it. This is the basis on which this world thrives. The population explosion is the direct consequence of this love.

Neil and Anita sat squeezing each other's hand. Even the air between the palms of their hands felt the tight hold and withdrew in a hurry so that it doesn't get annihilated. The red blood corpuscles [RBC] had already scurried away leaving in its trail a white hand turned whiter.

The lead guitarist had strummed and the percussionist had made his presence felt for all couples to ease out of their chairs so that their weight would be off the legs (of the chairs) and it would breathe more easily.

The M.C.'s words were spilling out like a silken thread of web floating in the light breeze pulling the grey suited boys, the black, the brown and the dark blue suits onto the wooden floor which creaked with ecstasy. All these tailor-made suits had an affinity for a particular brand of umbrella-cut pink frock or was it the six-piece sky blue frock billowing in the air? Were the boys the Pied-Pipers of Hamelin for as they stretched their right hands, the girls just drifted towards them like the South Pole of a magnet pulling the North Pole of another.

The lights in the hall had gone dim as though they were tired shining and doing 'kawwa-pari' (Keeping a watch) whole night. The darker got the hall, the slower became the drum-beats as though the drummer couldn't find the skin of the taut drums. It was certainly not a waltz but a Slow-Fox-Trot that the couples were dancing to. The incandescent bulbs refused to light up as though shy of the scene below to reveal the locked lips of some who shuddered and yet clung on. The chests heaved with excitement and there was a tingling sensation that only someone who is in love can feel the exuberance of. The masculine gender from Mars held on to his Eve with all the muscles that he could crush her with and the lady from Venus grasped him tight with all her tenderness for she still rules the roost. There was an eerie hush in the hall—even the wooden floor refused to creak for fear it may disturb the inseparables. The gossip-mongers seemed to be part of the crowd for the empty chairs heaved a sigh of relief for just carrying their own light weight though a sneer on their faces could not be wiped out and was still palpable.

"Is this going to be our last dance or will we meet again?" "Promise me you will hold me like this always" as he crushed her loving, longing delicate hands in his manly grip.

Even the M.C. had left his high pedestal to stoop to conquer a pretty, bubbly, swanky young girl who showed opulence in her frilly dress and looked frank in her opinion of herself.

All were cuddled in their own dark corners, the unabashed right in the middle of the dance floor caring 'two hoots' about the gazing Janes and peeping Toms. However, the whole crowd was on the dance floor nudging and pushing each other inadvertently. Nobody seemed to mind who was touching who or suddenly came in their way for tongues were pouring out their lava of love into the cauldron of ears; the pupils of the eyes closing to a slit so that the extra light stayed out and did not dilute the density and intensity of their love for each other. The sinews and muscles of the arms gave the delicate girls the protection that they looked for in a man. What trait distinguishes a girl from a lady is their independent nature that they vehemently throw around later in life.

The lead guitarist's eyes are normally perpetually closed whether he sleeps through 'Dr. Zhivago's Somewhere my love' while playing or sleeps through his play, was and is a theme for research. Anyway, let not the bogies of our story derail. One invincible rhythm guitarist who played through the night still had, though the sun never played peek-a-boo with the dawn, music flowing from the strings of his guitar whether it was G-major or any other chord that he strummed, hid the faltering notes of 'the forty winks' guitarist which otherwise is also not noticeable to the common ear except the seasoned musician.

To make a dramatic ending, the M.C. in a choked voice was adding 'all good things must come to an end—adieu, sayonara, gute nacht, bye-bye and fizzled out.

The grown-up lads and lasses, the girls and boys, one-night-stand couples, the kissing couples, the ever-loving husband and wife and the future ones who would tie-the-knot on the altar just melted away like the glaciers melting in the Antarctica. The dense fog that enveloped the city refused to reveal even the receding silhouettes of the couples like Gogia Pasha, the magician, would make 'the Statue of Liberty', disappear.

Words had to be hammered out of Neil and Anita for they clung to each other like a mother to her child. Kisses came in like Sachin Tendulkar's hundred and caresses like a baker's dozen, both unwilling to let go first. In a foreign country, Indians, including myself, become more unabashed than are the foreigners themselves. The restraining finger of the Indian fathers, the screwed-up eyes of the mother and the rolled-up brows of the gossiping neighbours makes the teens shun such liberty.

When in Rome do as the Romans do, we Indians love to follow proverbs to the hilt and Neil and Anita were no different. In a one-night stand, Anita and Neil had shaped up like Siamese twins; they had become so obsessed with each other as though they knew each other for years together. Being of a shy nature and difficult to open up with strangers, Anita had not responded to the prying eyes of the fair-skinned boys. It was not conceit but her introvert nature that inspite of her innermost desire to be wanted by someone, to be touched by someone she had only whispered 'yes' or 'no' to the boy's query. She had languished in her jail of thoughts and desires and never let them get aired in the sunshine, to let them blossom along with the primroses and the daisies of the field.

On the other hand, Neil was almost the opposite, ready to burst into laughter at the flimsiest excuse, ready to join in any conversation with replies that had a scientific temper and was with the children and almost a mother to the oldies. What fascinated him the most were girls above sweet sixteen and below twenty-one, his terrain of thoughts very similar to any young normal boy in college.

Neil and Anita's love at first sight was like instant coffee. One night of dancing was churning out a life-size fairy tale dream into reality. Many times through the night while dancing Anita had asked "Neil pinch me". She had screamed in a low profile "it's real, it's true".

All those who have been through this maze of love will discern the magnanimity it holds. The world looks like a Santa Claus distributing gifts of love, a kaleidoscope of only soft eyes and soft feelings towards all and bereft of any hard-heartedness. What is this love? It is difficult to assign a place to it especially if you have never been through this whirlwind of love.

Neil's friends had finished off with their new girl-friends and were hunting for him to return to Germany from Luxembourg which was just a few kilometers drive away.

"Come on, come on, let's get moving" but Neil's ears were not tuned to theirs for it fell on deaf ears. It was quite a challenge for them to pull Anita and Neil apart who were busy giving and taking promises. Both were of the opinion that God had created this channel to come all the way from India and meet here. What God wanted to join let no man put asunder. With this conviction, with a terribly heavy heart both pulled themselves from each other but to meet very soon. Names and addresses were already exchanged and armed with these, what a sight it was still to see them depart. Have you seen a small wailing child being pulled away from the mother? The scene was almost identical only there was no free flow of the salty tears but eyes were moist which did not leave the sight of each other till the receding taxis disappeared in the fog.

No Man's Land

The taxis sped over the tarred roads. The tyres screeching and murmuring in whispers to its life-long friend, the road. The cars and roads clung onto each other like a wife clings onto her husband, slipping on the curves of the road as a lover's hand moving smoothly on the body of his beloved. See the temperament of the road behaving like a wife when angry giving a cold shoulder and a berating tongue knowing fully well when she pushes the car off the road—all accidents occur on curves.

Neil's friends were busy talking of the exploits of the night. How they shivered and shook with each new girl, for every dance, making herself cozy with them. Every dance they felt 'this was the girl for them' which vanished with a shimmer at the next dance. The boys looked for their old dancing partners but the girls in the arms of another were oblivious and indifferent to their cajoling eyes and entreaties. The boys for a fleeting moment felt dejected and crest-fallen, only the softness of the hand at 98.4 degrees Fahrenheit which they were holding now, brought them back to reality and they basked and soaked themselves in the coziness of the girl who clung to them like Ivy. Any normal Indian guy like me or even Asian would feel happy 'better a bird in hand than two in the bush'.

I can't, for certain, put the same yard-stick for any other.

The air in the taxi was charged and crisp with red bloodied boys thinking of girls in yellow frilly frocks which would turn to orange at the mere touch (VIBGYOR) or any other myriad colour. Normally boys and girls fall for the first pair of legs they see or the first pair of pants especially if they were far away from their parent's homes or the mother-father not too close. This I can say for certainty for myself and zero percent for others who would, anyway, corroborate my so well rehearsed theory.

Normally girls keep their heads on their shoulders and know what they want and go tong and chisel after it. Somehow, today, Anita's head was swirling in a pool of chaos. She otherwise was such a cool girl. While travelling from Lahore (undivided India) few months earlier, she had never held any boy's hand for a dance or even dreamt of such a fantasy. Today she was standing dangling precariously on the edge of a precipice wondering whether to turn back or swim through the proverbial seven seas for her first love. Love like water is so wonderful when you swim in it and so treacherous when it takes the form of a tsunami. Her mother's beseeching eyes, flooded with tears, trying her level best to keep the sluice-gates of the dam from bursting. No letting Tom, Dick and Harry know about Anita's departure from India was a closed guarded secret. The spilling of the salty water from her almond shaped eyes would only reveal all and neighbours and close relatives would harbour evil wishes which would come in her way of success, so they all believed.

One thing was certain she was madly in love—love at first sight, no, no love at first night of dancing. She could feel Neil's hot, humid hands in hers still. She could feel his shallow breathing turn to heavy as he pulled her closer in his vice-like grip. The aroma of the perfume he wore still filled her nostrils and she was in no hurry to say bye to it. It was goading her into an exhilarating feeling of nostalgia. Her voluptuous torso heaved with every thought of him. Neil had formed a frame of halo all around her and there was no escape but who the hell wanted to run from him. She wanted time to stand still and Neil to cover her tight as would a blanket on a cold winter night. The thought of her mum and dad that troubled her day in and day out had taken a back-seat and the frugal ones that had the audacity to freak in were nudged out of her head politely but firmly. She wanted to be draped only with Neil's love. It was like a mother's love for her child—everything in this world has to wait when a child's hunger has to be quenched. This only a mother or a lover who has been through this agony of ecstasy will understand. Railway junctions can come and go but I stick to only one track, that of Neil's, all other railway lines are either merged to the main Neil's line or pass off as a blur like the abandoned houses. Every thought of him only brought an upheaval in her life and now nothing would endear to soothe her nerves. Unobtrusively her mind played games with her-one minute in the abyss of happiness and exhilaration and second minute in the parched land of the Sahara desert, helpless and forlorn with no one in sight except the sifting sand-dunes overtly showing the mirage of the oasis.

The screeching of the brakes was like the tyre and the road at cross-roads with each other complaining of the heat generated between them. Anita's reverie was broken. The clouds of Neil's thoughts that hovered over her like a helicopter just vanished. Welcoming her was the gate that had let her in and out thousands of time by standing ajar. It was cold to the touch but warmth flowed when it welcomed her in.

Girls encircled her as she entered the dormitory with queries 'How was the show?' 'Did some handsome boy come her way?' Interview over, Anita tried to sleep but could she? Her thoughts ran back to the dancing hall.

How Neil had squeezed her in his manly arms and how she had squirmed only wanting him to hold her tighter in his vice-like grip. The whole scene of the night before flooded her. How Neil had bowed and asked her for the first dance, a tremor ran through her body as he touched her. Is this what people call love at first sight or is it the hunger when one climbs the ladder of adulthood? If you have the same craving for all men then it is lust but if it is only for Neil it is love.

On the quiet Neil sat in the taxi smelling his left hand which had unwittingly absorbed "The Night in Paris perfume" from Anita's hand. His friends kept on talking while the taxi's engine purred with delight at the answers Neil murmured without understanding much. His thoughts swarmed with the intoxicating love for Anita.

Something was burning. Was jealously? It could be, for pervading the air was a burnt smell of rubber (of the tyre) on the tarred road, wheels had got stuck on the road like two lips locked in a kiss.

With difficulty, the friends pulled out Neil from the car whose hand was still close to his nostrils savouring Anita's perfume. The guard on duty woke Neil and his friends from their slumber when he asked them to produce their written permission to cross over to Luxembourg. They had none and their God-Father guard was off-duty. They were standing on 'No-man's land' between the borders of Germany and Luxembourg. The earth under their feet seemed to have collapsed. The five senses they were so proud of refused to budge even with all their coaxing. They were just stunned. 'What will happen and what were they supposed to do?' 'Will they be hand-cuffed and imprisoned for violating the law?' No one had any answers. They only drew solace from the fact that they were not alone and all stood together thick as thieves. When they saw policemen passing and re-passing, some with hand-cuffs in their hand, they felt they were coming for them and they shivered and shook in their pants. Their nerves were shattered and they did not have the spine to acknowledge that they were so stupid as not to arm themselves with passports etc. This is youth and such mistakes will re-occur anywhere, anytime. I hope the oldies, the officers and the Ambassadors in the embassies all over the world will peep down the drain-pipes (of the pants) of their youth and pass it off without giving that stern, stiff look.

Imagine Hitler as the Head and Dictator of Germany in whose mouth butter must be refusing to melt, in such a scenario Indian Embassy in Frankfurt was called on, to vouch for these four Indian 'ladlas' (Darlings) of their mothers. Great was their rejoicing when after 3-4 hours in No-Man's land they were given permission to cross over to Germany.

The four gloated over their fate. God had been kind to let them off so easily from the clutches and tentacles of the law. All shuddered and shook. Neil was the first to forget the embarrassment they had gone through in the 'No Man's land'. He had no choice for better pursuits in life than the one at present which attracted him like a moth to a flame. Anita had come like a whirlwind and swept him off his feet. His nostrils widened to smell the aroma of Anita's perfume lingering on his hands, like bees with their superior olfactory sense fly to the nectar of the wild daises. It would be hard to believe that this activity, absurd to millions of readers, continued for full three days. Some readers would be hesitant to believe. 'Why, didn't Neil visit the wash-room and then weren't his hands washed?' Only Neil was in a position to answer that query but those who have nose-dived into the magnanimity of love will understand that everything is possible when two hearts ache for each other.

The seeds of love were sown on the wooden dancing floors of Luxembourg. Signs of sprouting had already shown its evidence. Whether it would grow into a huge tree with branches and tendrils shooting and buds blossoming into Magnolia flowers with their lovely hue would be discernable only with time. It could also wither away as do a lot of love stories that begin with each step that softness of Venus melts in the muscles of the man from Mars and then as the dance fades so does the memory of the person. A wonderful way the human psyche works to weed out the unwanted. A person you can spend a few hours for pleasure but not for a lifetime.

Anita and Neil's story was written in letters of gold, maybe in the Almighty's hand itself. One side Anita was sighing with agony and the other side Neil was cooing for love like a dove.

Neil was not the only boy in the world who had dreamt and yearned for female company with statistics of 36-24-36 with carnal desires. But today, mathematics of numbers had just faded and he was looking through a glazed glass only at a silhouette when he wanted to touch, feel, speak and see his gazelle shaped eyes pouring her woes and agony into the antennae of his ears without having to even open her pouting, kissable lips. The husky, cool voice that emanated from the velvety, suave tongue on very few occasions through-out the night preferred to stay indoors, inside the cave of her mouth where the adorable lips act as sentries and are both polite and harsh with their kiss and hiss, applicable mostly for the slender gender. She can be as gentle as a mother and yet as ferocious as a tigress when her children are in danger. Gentlemen beware while coaxing a girl to be your wife, put a few obstacles in her way and hell will pour forth from her nasty tongue, vocabulary that even Oxford dictionary would hesitate to print on its pages. Run if you can and seek solace on another soft padded shoulder.

I couldn't be one sided for there are endless girls who are not just ivory beautiful, but beautiful in their thoughts, words and deeds. If you come across this rare species just get her to the altar and spin a ring around her finger; she'll be the miss who didn't miss being a Mrs. (misses).

The boys in their sophomore years at college felt they knew almost everything about Germany and its surroundings by now had got acclimatized to the weather like the Germans and the Europeans. They forgot they were Indians and had to drink brandy instead of the lager beer in the dance hall.

UPS and Downs of Life

As all the four boys tried rolling out of bed, they felt feverish. Their heads swirled and their bodies had involuntary shivers. When the boys were shifted to the college-hospital, three were diagnosed by the doctor with severe cold which if untreated would culminate into pneumonia and Neil, above all, had malaria. Not a very nice time for God Almighty to shower him with such ailments when he wanted to be out clasping Anita's hand and pouring out adjectives by the hundred even those that did not exist in Webster's dictionary. Mushrooming of the mobile had not taken place as it is now for it was not born in those days. So the only alternative was to take recourse of the pen and paper. Neil wrote this letter to Anita, the girl he felt, he could not live without.

My one and only one, darling Anita, My silence must have shaken the very foundations of faith and promises, your rivulet of tears is knocking on my door seeking for an answer.

At the dance hall while we were sipping lager beer, the mosquitoes had put their straw in the human-cold drink-bottle, that's your Neil and drank to their heart's content the red blood that oozed out of the pipe. As a parting and return-party gift they left behind the malaria bacteria. In crisp, bold letters I could and can see the words floating that they left behind 'Thank you for the drinks—Your Uninvited Guests, The Mosquitoes'.

From the writing you can make out how I shiver and shake. I have a cold feeling running down my spine. It's only the warmth from your lacerated thoughts that I solicit and draw energy to write this dilapidated letter.

As the Holy Book says the spirit is willing but the flesh is weak, so is my case. Still I will not gnash my teeth, nor will I frown at the Almighty for it was HE who brought the impeccable Anita to my arms and I will not refrain from acceding to His demands.

I was a boy who would go for a wedding party and when the priest in his sonorous voice would declare the boy and girl to be legally married as husband and wife. 'What GOD has joined let no man put asunder'—'otherwise from her side will come thunder'. Peals of subdued laughter would emanate from around me in a circle for I was the atheist who had echoed such incoherent words in an audible whisper.

Sheaves of pages in our computer brain that jots down every emotion, every lingering thought and engraves it for eternity looks shrouded and erased since I met my tantalizing beauty, Anita. Peep into the mirror and astonishingly you will find its constant gaze on my Anita's beauty. Be careful walls have ears, but mirrors have even eyes, and sure, all have heard of the talking mirror.

What a deadly combination; beware if it lets out the cat and your innermost secrets or lets out the skeletons out of your cupboard on which it (mirror) is securely fastened. Now, now come out of it, I was just pulling your legs. Still check if one leg hasn't become longer than the other? Ha, ha, ho, ho, he, he.

This was just to keep agony out of your way and let happiness creep our way. What, under your breath you called me a creep? Sorry, it was my own conscience troubling me.

It seems I'm already recuperating from the onslaught of malaria. Is it your capsules of love or the pills of quinine the doctor prescribed? 'Sleep tight, don't let the bed-bugs bite'. Anita, did you send your swarm of mosquitoes to disarm you from the tentacles of other girls prying like the mantis on innocent boys, like Neil.

My prowess at making you laugh may have failed but my penchant to be in a cohesive society of smiling faces remains—incorrigible as ever.

Not once did my fingers show signs of creaking pain; not once did my mouth stop reading what my heart dictated; not once did my tongue groan a Ooh! Or Aah!

Inspite of the raging malarial temperature of 105 degrees Fahrenheit and the internal inferno of your love, close I must and close I will before my dam of patience bursts and I come running to cling to your loving arms.

Forever Yours,
Neil.

Love Birds

Two days later, there was a gentle knock on the door and when Neil answered that the door was open and for the usherer to walk in, the wooden door creaked with Heavenly bliss at the touch of the delicate, ivory fingers. The door stood ajar and two sparkling, moist, doe-eyes took in the scenario of the ruffled bed sheet and in the midst of the bed the rumpled, shriveled figure of Neil in disarray. It was like the North Pole of one magnet attracting the South Pole of another magnet. What happened next was a jig-saw puzzle that any married or even an un-married couple would guess and chances are they would be almost 200 percent correct. The birds and the bees do it and almost anything that crawls on this earth, does it. God himself said 'Go and multiply' and now that we have passed the Abacus stage and moved onto the chip in a mobile in each and every hand, even a rickshaw puller knows nature's way of population explosion.

Readers will have to excuse me for not leading them to the explicit scenes for which they desire most in life.

I must confess even I was deprived of such an intimacy between Neil and Anita. I just saw Anita and Neil holding each other sitting in a cloud with a silver lining and another tantalizing opaque curtain to keep me out of this Heavenly bliss and my bleary-eyed readers.

When all the excitement of the activity was over, the curtain was lifted and two exhausted lovers with every vestige of energy drained could be seen lying dormant and motionless. They had violated Indian culture by intruding into forbidden territory.

It was Anita who ran her fragile fingers on Neil's face, ruffled his hair and in her suave voice murmured, "I'll get some hot drink for my baby and is it time for your medicines?" Neil was in the seventh heavens to find such a charming, vivacious, cultured and caring girl looking after him when he needed someone the most.

After Neil had the cup of hot milk, Anita went reconnoitering the room and found the fruit basket. She hadn't eaten a morsel when Neil's letter was delivered to her. She now peeled a banana for she was ravenous. The banana felt ashamed half clad, half naked. To save it's embarrassment she hid a part of it in the cavity of her mouth and chewed on it. Slowly she had devoured the rest and the banana peels shaking like the grass-skirts of Hawaiian girls in her hand were put to rest in the empty dustbin with no one for company.

Happy Days Are Here Again

It was a lovely day in Frankfurt. The rains had come and gone leaving in its trail sparkling green leaves on the trees, absolutely dust free. The flowers looked drunk swaying in the gentle breeze as would a man who has had drinks by the gallons—A sight neighbours and strangers love and home-people just hate.

I personally feel the mud in which all these flowers bloom must be full of colours. Why see the yellow of the Marigold; the white of the Lilies rupturing out of the brown manure; the purple spilling out of the pansies with the yellow skirting around it to hold it, back; tulips brought from Holland defying all colours and pasting the petals with every vibrant hue. The rose hewn from the parent stem and nurtured in the mud with dry leaves shows-off with buds that open up like chrysalis bursts to let a butterfly of diverse shades to fly out. The rose with all the scintillating colours and a perfume to match is rightly called the king of flowers. Who else but his majesty would have security guards all around-the Thorns.

Enough of nature and greenery let us come back to the most important flower of all that this mother Earth has provided. They come in all shapes and sizes. The Tom-Thumbs, the dwarfs, the so-called average and those blessed with gigantism and then the black, the fair, the brown, the very fair, fair with pink rubbed all over, the ugly, the not-so-ugly, pretty, beautiful, handsome and the stunning beauty—all inherit this earth. They are endowed with stilts in the shape of number eleven (11) with roving buttons that could glimpse anything, with antennae that could track any sound, two palm shaped leaves attached to two bamboos which show their whims and fancies by striking or embracing at will, a motor that works constantly for around 70-80 years, pumping red wine through canals intoxicating this colossal into believing there is no one above till the machine splutters and stops and then it is too late to relent. There is yet something the shape of the kernel of the walnut where Angel Gabriel and the devil reside. Both keep puncturing the conscience into temptation for good and evil. Normally the silky, amorous, ichy-rich path of the evil is more soothing and followed by both the curvy and muscular species—yes, people like you and me.

NOTE:

1. Stilts with number 11—legs
2. Roving buttons—your eyes
3. Antennae—Ears
4. Two palm shaped leaves with two bamboos—two hands and two arms.
5. Motor—Heart
6. Red wine—Blood
7. Kernel of the walnut—Brain
8. Curvy and muscular species—woman and man

Now, now where have we left Neil and Anita? Yes both are very much with us except that we gave time for Neil to recuperate fully from malaria of which people used to dread in those days as they do today of dengue which also is brought in by the mosquito, yes Aides mosquito which is effective only below 17 degrees centigrade and normally strikes in the day-time.

Anita had looked after Neil till he recovered fully and now they could not live without each other. They were so attached as is a postage stamp to the envelope.

They would go on long rides on his bicycle, Anita sitting on the rod of the cycle in-front of him. On one such sojourn Neil took six oranges in a plastic bag and hung it on the handle of the cycle to be eaten on the way. She kept telling him the whole day's incidents while peeling the oranges one after another and feeding him. Rapt attention was what he paid to every sentence she unfurled from her tongue while his eyes delved deeper and deeper into her eyes to discern their colour. Many a times he would forget that they were on the road and nearly miss some passerby who would acknowledge the near-miss with a smile. Such good days can one dream of now? He and even she wondered if they left India to find each other in Germany. The gold-rush in Johannesburg in South Africa was nothing spectacular compared to the eternal love they found in each other. When the brakes of the cycle came to action, Anita jumped off the rod and teasingly asked him "How were the six oranges?" And he woke up to the truth that she had been feeding him the oranges and he was so happy with his arm full of dreams that no other thoughts even ventured to come near, even that she had not tasted the fruit but only the fruit of love. She was the luckiest to have a bellyful.

Neil scratched his head to find out what he wanted to tell Anita and like Gogia Pasha doing magic it came running to him. Someone who was celebrating their silver wedding anniversary was throwing a party and invited both of them to come.

Black Monday arrived with a lot of fear and trepidation and lots of work which had piled over Saturday and

Sunday. The little left-over was pushed for Tuesday to finish but the unending lectures by the professors made their interesting work reach new dimensions. Thursday was no better but Friday as hectic as ever, brought in a ray of hope for Saturday, inspite of all the hurdles in its way, always follows Friday. Come what may, it tip-toes after it.

Chivalrous as ever, Neil took the lead in letting Anita enter the house first of the good Samaritans. What if the dog was loose and not on its leash? Anita could stave off the attack on him. Good way, my dear boy to be a stickler for manners—'Ladies First'—Equality had taken a back seat when the need arises.

My dear readers I was just pulling your legs. (Of course, I have a suggestion to make. When you lie in bed tonight just check if one leg is not longer than the other. Sick joke did you say? Laugh heartily and live happily).

The host and hostess received all the guests with rare warmth intermixed with loud laughter and didn't look the forty-nine and fifty-two years that they claimed and drummed it into each one of the guests.

"I would like my guests to roar in our excitement, my wife's and mine, and enjoy every minute of the evening. The three storeys of the almond-sugar cake tells us the three stories of our affa—" and the wife's hand and then her lips sealed his mouth with her kiss—she didn't want her linen to be washed in public.

From somewhere 'Congratulations and Celebration' music started and the dear, divine twenty-five year old married bride-groom picked his quarter-century old bride by the hand and swept her across the floor in the traditional wedding march followed by the cheering, dancing guests.

Small wine glasses showed their existence with their clinking and clanging and that they were full to the brim with wine, and excitement would topple it over to spill the red contents on the floor to let it share their happiness with a drink or two.

The bride-groom was up again with a glass of wine in his hand to give the toast. He asked everyone to clap loud. "There are so many claps hidden in the palms of your hand, just unleash them" and everyone gave a hand.

For Brown and Pussy—25 years of Silver lining

Honey-Moon brings its teething trouble,
Then it just vanishes like a bubble
Like Mount Vesuvius it dormant stays,
And erupts as sudden and lava sprays.
Tired and twisted the twenty-six alphabets rest
To give it shape the Hindi dictionary flaps.
The tongue lashing over it goes in its cave,
To bounce back to life in its kitchen enclave

Brown and Pussy, what to say are with knives and cutlery in each other's way.
Guns and pistols were swung each day as I shiver in my pants today.
A slithery motion of wet I feel,
Could it be that, what do you say?
Hell-on-Earth on my door has never witnessed a day,
What I told was just a dream, far, far away.

There was a resounding, thunderous applause and everyone fell to talking in whispers, that were loud enough for all to hear, about the words that were selected and were they true to the couple's life, did he steal the words from some book, he doesn't have the capacity to write such words that fit so beautifully into the right slots and then the needle of the H.M.V. (His Master's Voice) Record-Player was on the grooves of the record pulling out lovely, lilting music which turned out to be Lara's Theme and everyone pulled their partners for a soothing waltz.

Another waltz and a slow-fox-trot set the pace and then gentlemen to the Bar and ladies to the Cloak-room, someone announced. There was almost a queue for the 'bitter drinks' that the poor men are forced to drink in the name of courtesy and being social.

There was also a rush towards the ladies-room which is the favourite place for the fairer-sex. Smudged lip-sticks had to be re-touched and smacked. Dresses had to be adjusted-readjusted.

I have hardly spoken about Neil and Anita. Both were busy holding each other tight as though Neil wanted to put an imprint of his on Anita and vice-versa. Promises of tomorrow were being made and sealed and stamped with a kiss while they gyrated to the lilting music.

The dance was in full swing when the music was stopped and a deep throated voice rang out. Ladies and gentleman, this dance will continue as a competition-Newspaper Folding Dance Competition. Pages of newspaper were distributed and observers placed at strategic places. Couples had to put the paper on the floor and dance on it without touching the floor. Music was again stopped and the newspaper folded in half. The music would once again be pilfered from the grooves of the records and siphoned off into the waiting hall via the needle of the record player.

The couples would jump onto the receding area of the newspaper with excitement trying not to touch the floor. In the beginning all danced comfortably, till the newspaper was folded five-six times. You could see the observers pulling up the couples who even slightly touched the floor to sit down. Some couples would laugh heartily and take to their seats sportingly; others would giggle and take to their seats quietly; yet there were just a few who had to be coerced into sitting for they felt they hadn't touched the floor and reluctantly left for their seats with a sneer on their faces.

Only four couples were basking in this arena of stability with success when the newspaper fold had taken the size of their toes. Every boy had lifted the girl up in the air who clung to them like a creeper. The boys gave the appearance of a stork in a field standing on one leg.

Everyone watched with bated breath the taut figures that brought in all their gymnastic and athletic skills they possessed. Neil and Anita were very much in the competition. Anita and even the other girls, three to be precise, had discarded their shoes and were standing on the tips of the boy's toes who had turned into statues with one leg flailing in the air. It seemed lightning had struck the party for there was a whirr and flash of the cameras. It was a sight worth capturing for the couples looked like swans in an invisible oasis of water.

Every eye of the onlookers had narrowed to a slit, some unabashedly saying the 'Our Father' for their friends not to flinch a muscle like 'Statue of Liberty' stands motionless for years. Neil's eyes dug deep into Anita's pupil and he saw her eyes penetrating into his with an indescribable love that only lovers can fathom. They were holding each other and yet were far away to maintain the equilibrium and to keep their centre of gravity as low as possible for stability, hadn't they seen trucks carrying heavy loads piled to the top and yet happily trudging along. The dainty darlings hung onto the trunks of the trees, so the boys seemed, while their frocks fluttered like a flag, teasing the eager eyes of the onlookers from catching a glimpse of what it concealed one moment and what it revealed the next. It looked like the Russian ballerinas on their skates had descended the scene only this time they were almost stationary. It looked like the clock stood still and yet it was ticking away till it looked like eternity and then two of the boy's legs just revolted and sank as though the marrow was drained out of their bones. Both the couples to hide their embarrassment laughed and glided away into a remote corner, far away from the scathing and searing eyes of the critics who blossom like locusts everywhere.

All this time Neil was swimming in Anita's eyes and she in his. The other couples pant and skirt were straining to come closer to each other and in so doing the magnetic pull of the floor pulled the pant and skirt down along with their owners. The crowd went berserk with 'Neil, Anita; Neil, Anita' for they had caught the fancy of most of the people there. Neil and Anita were the undisputed Prince and Princess of the Newspaper Competition.

It was a lovely day in the company of lovely people. It was a day to be treasured long after Neil and Anita were married with their children playing in the court-yard of their Home sweet Home. Possibly a few streaks of white hair would adorn Anita's head like a crown justifying she was still the princess of this prince, Neil. Neil would, in all probability, cup Anita's chin in his cupped hands and kiss her nose and then her closed eyes which were filled with satiated love to the brim and yet endearing him for more. The cup of love can never be full even when the froth of love is brimming over and running down the sides of the wall. Lucky are those couples who get inebriated in this sojourn of love and yet cling onto their partners as though they have just seen a pair of passionate eyes all afire, for the first time, and like the moth would like to kindle themselves in this warmth.

Anita and Neil were basking in this unperturbed world of love where hundreds of vehicles may have passed on the road outside, with their ear-splitting noise and blood curdling speeds. All this fretting and fuming of the cars and buses, soft lands on the ears of the lovers like whispers. What is evident to them is the cajoling and the cooing of each other. All the frequencies on a frequency modulated (F.M.) radio with their jarring music are off, so is 'Radio Francis', only the channel of love is attuned and so there is no disturbing news or music which would stifle Anita and Neil's gurgling love story.

"What a lovely evening, I'll treasure it for life" whispered Anita in Neil's ear.

Both Anita and Neil did not miss any opportunity to be together as far as their studies did not suffer.

Not Everest, But Alps in Their Laps

It is natural for children to play with toys, dolls for the girls and ball for the boys. As he assumes adulthood he plays with lively, shapely girls. He just cannot sit still. When married, he plays with smiling, innocent babies and takes pride in putting their diapers. His world has shrunk to his wife and children and he waits to hear the first time his child calls him 'da-da'.

Anita's college boys and girls were going for an excursion to Berne, Switzerland. Neil joined them on Anita's insistence and he simply loved and relished being coerced into it.

Neil in his dreams saw the meandering Alps high and lofty and snuggled to him was his warmth, his palpitation, his Anita. Her thoughts hovered around him like a helicopter, only did not raise so much dust as it did his craving for her. He had forgotten living for himself. He just lived to see that mischievous smile adorning her face. Both had decided to raise all the dust of happiness they could before they lay down and the dust on them. Oh! My, my, why did his thoughts even linger for a second close to the graveyard? This is the beauty of our minds, one split second on the thorny red rose with one leg in the grave and the next second like a butterfly on a carnation.

We talk of Kashmir as the Switzerland of India. Even one of the Mughal Emperors of India had pronounced that if there was a paradise on earth it was in Kashmir since I'm available on the subject and having spent almost 15-20 days there for my wife's honey-moon and my money-moon, (Ha, ha—I just wanted a streak of that constipated laugh slip my wife's lips) I can vouch anyone who has not been there must get their visas and passport ready and book the next flight. There will be no disappointment but you could drool at the mouth seeing the beauty of the place.

At the moment, the itinerary of the bus carrying college boys and girls was Stuttgart, Strasbourg and ultimately Berne, Switzerland. Practically all the hundred feet or so, both left and right legs, were firmly ensconced on the floor of the bus. Two feet strayed away, one left and one right, and were consistently rubbing against each other like two tentacles. They drew warmth and energy from each other and were confined to pressing against each other and the magic potion of love oozed out into each other. They were the legs of Anita and Neil as they sat squeezed up in almost one seat when two were available for both. Five fingers of each hand did not know the limitations of the area that they could titillate. It was difficult to say whether Anita's or Neil's hands had manoeuvred more or less, territory of each other. The juicy lips just sought each other's company and were sealed as though 'Glue' had found its way in between the crevices and cemented them together.

Had such a scene occurred in any other country, some neighbours would have shut their eyes in shame, occasionally opening their eye-lids stealthily to soak in the scene and pilfer it in their mind's eye for eternity. Others would blatantly cry shame but heart to heart would love to exchange places with Neil and Anita.

The very old generation who have now developed 'Rhino Skin' and have no feelings towards a touch are the ones who would be outright in their condemnation. 'Neigh-bours' are rightly called so as they 'neigh'(talk) like horses about people living next door, good or bad—mostly bad that will blaspheme the neighbour.

The driver of the bus was a sturdy, young fellow whose consistent smile from east to west drew all and sundry like a moth to a flame. His smile was contagious and all the college boys and girls in the bus were a happy lot. 'Cheerio here I go on my way' was lustily sung by the inmates of the bus, while the bus tyres in association with the most contagious music director, 'The Tarred Road' gave it' s own back ground music-uh, uh, uh, uh. It is certain whatever passes, whether a truck, a car, a limousine over the road's chest, belly or even legs, it produces a regular background music of its own.

Leave the blistering music alone and let's peek-a-boo inside the bus. The atmosphere was as congenial as we had left it. It had become a breeding ground for laughter and fun. The boys and girls sang with a sweet tongue full of gusto.

There was a joke doing the rounds that Leila, who was so thin and frail, could be sucked into the nostrils of the boy sitting behind her, if he breathed a little harder. What a flurry of laughter echoed through the bus that it nearly burst at the seams. Fortunately the bus was reinforced with steel and withstood the catastrophe or else all the boys and girls would have spilled onto the roads. I wonder what music comes out when you rub human strings on the road? Frowning music from the girls and utterly butterly disastrous music from the boys, I suppose.

Every small halt had piping hot coffee and snacks making in-roads into the bus. Everyone was in high spirits waiting for the first glimpse of the silhouette of the Alps.

Most of the boys and girls had got out of the bus to stretch their legs and to see how it was outside. Did the wind tear you apart or was it a gentle breeze kissing your curls and making you drowsy? Anita and Neil sat glued to their seat admiring the works of the Lord, Anita admiring the handsome Neil and Neil loved all baby girls above sixteen years and especially now was engrossed in a girl spelt A-n-i-t-a. He couldn't come to terms that such a charming, lovely, educated girl was all his, who wouldn't bother to throw glances anywhere else. Anita on her part reposed full trust in Neil and never doubted his sincerity. She was his and he hers entirely.

The stipulated half-an-hour stop was over. The weight of the bus in one position for 30 minutes had punched holes in the tarred road. The headache that all the passing vehicles gave it (road) seemed a little relieved with the pressing. As the bus rolled on with all the passengers intact the road heaved a sigh of relief and wished the bus 'adieu and a big thank you.'

The tyres and the road sang their own tune of their long association with each other, while the inmates of the bus just let the music pass from one ear and out from the other. God's kindness in providing two ears was so conspicuous here. I always laughed why God gave us two nostrils till I found one nostril clogged with cold.

The spirits of the lasses and their counterparts had not abated and they were up in arms with a game 'Passing the Chocolate'. They had to pass this mouth-watering chocolate to their immediate neighbour who would pass to the next while sitting in their seats. The chocolate was gift wrapped atleast five times. As the music stopped the parcel was in Leila's hand. With trepidation she gingerly opened one layer and found a slip 'Sing a Song'. From the petite body which could hardly hold a quarter of a litre of water came a resounding, honey dipped voice which just a few would have ever discerned to connect with the frail Leila. Many jumped up to save her from flying out of the window. Her diaphragm stood the test of time with the verve of her undulating tune. There was a look of pleasant surprise on every occupant of the bus, with the driver joining in at the fag end of the song with the hilarious nature of his voice.

Nobody could believe their eyes or ears and were agog at how Sheila sang. The music started and the parcel was on its rounds like a policeman. The music stopped as the parcel reached Lucy's hands but she had pushed it away in the nick of time as she said and it now swayed in Pakori Lal's hands. Boys being chivalrous, Pakori Lal took up the challenge. He undid the gift once more and found the piece of paper directing him to stand on his hands. Everyone was dismayed, especially the girls, for they really wanted Lucy to stand on her hands and see her six piece frock falling onto her shoulders like the petals of the Hibiscus flower opening up. It would have been a lovely scene to watch but knowing Lucy; perhaps the boys feeling ashamed would have turned their faces away but not before getting a passing glimpse.

Pakori Lal was not dismayed at the directions of the chit in his hand. In fact he felt God had bestowed this favour on him. Many times, in the foot-ball field, he had shown his prowess by standing on his hands and sometimes on his head. The girls would be impressed. Just show me one boy who wouldn't want to show-off in front of the fairer sex.

Tarzan, it seems, had come to town. Nay, nay he was in the bus and in full view of the occupants of the bus, he put his hands down and up went his flailing legs in the air above his head. Instant rapt attention from his friends was at his disposal. Everyone was on their feet in the bus to give him a standing ovation and the claps that remain hidden in the palms of our hands were unleashed in full fury. There was no dearth of accolades but as we all know there's many a slip between the cup and the lip. The next moment the bus had swerved to avoid an accident with a speeding car which had come in its path. The ones who were applauding Pakori Lal went for a four while Pakori Lal went for a sixer. Their accolades did not go in vain for all had a narrow escape for Providence wanted it like that. The journey had started with a prayer and especially to St. Christopher for the safety of all. Their beseeching had been heard by the Almighty.

Hardly had the tyres thanked the road for holding it tight in its arms like a mother, when the driver fully recovered from the near-accident shock, took to the steering wheel. He drove in silence, unperturbed. It looked and sounded weird. It looked like this crowd of boys and girls sat on a thorny cactus and refused to whine in pain.

Soon the likes of a lovely place appeared. It was Stuttgart. The driver in his shrill, jovial voice announced "We are stopping for twenty minutes to stretch our legs. Those who wish to reach Berne will be back on time in the bus, Thank you."

Everybody trickled out of the bus except Anita and Neil. They were too busy talking of their future plans. They had decided they would get married as soon as they had finished their studies. They would be married in India with the blessings of their father and mother. Both had the same view about this but Anita wanted to live in India where as Neil preferred to come back to Germany. Such serious glimpses of talk can only filter out from people madly in love and they have to be head over Heels in love. How else would anyone talk like this except when the brain has given the power to the heart to think.

"Let's go and have a cup of hot coffee" whispered Anita, more with her raised and twisted eye-brows than her smudged lips from kissing. Hand in hand they walked out, happy as larks. They ordered two hot cups of coffee and two hamburgers. Slowly they sipped their coffee. While their lips dipped into their cups their eyes were totally immersed in each other's pupils and retinas. The hamburgers had the patience to wait endlessly for the two love-birds to dig their sparkling white teeth into them. When lions and tigers make love they snarl and bite the lionesses and tigresses respectively into submission. Perhaps the meat in the hamburger was not walking mutton—a live goat—but certainly had the traits of it and so was ready for the love-bites. In front of the intense love of Neil and Anita the hot cups of coffee were like a damp-squib and hardly anyone noticed their existence. Suddenly Neil pulled Anita's mesmerized hands, "drink your coffee dear and let's check how Stuttgart is?" whispered Neil in a hushed voice. Anita daintily lifted her cup and took a sip or two without any splurging noise, Neil did likewise and with the hamburgers in their hands they stepped out in the cool crisp air. There was no wind. Not even the slightest breeze or zephyr but the difference in temperature inside and out in the open did wake the two from their love-slumber. It was quite chill to be out. A Zeppelin would cajole them into going back but there was no airship not even the German one. The sun had refused to come out, maybe felt cold, took a blanket and slept off.

Inspite of the cold, Neil and Anita who were swathed in love, did not find their teeth chattering. They did not sprint, nor did they gallop or even canter but the CD (compact disc) of music was in their heads and hearts and if they wanted to dance to the tune of a Fox-Trot who could stop them. They walked on hand in hand and found themselves amidst flowers hewn out of the most vibrant material, which has colour, simplicity, built, you name it and it is there. The only thing you may forget to would be life. Yes, this Earth in the form of mud has produced this miracle called MAN, all kicking and full of life.

Let us come back to Earth and take out the thermometer to check the temperature of the warmth Anita and Neil were in.

Since Neil met Anita, he was never the normal 98.4 degrees F but seemed much hotter and the same was true for Anita. The scenery around them was breath-taking, simply picturesque. Both were lost in the beauty of the place and more so in the pleasantness of each other. When you are in love the pirates of Somalia would also look pleasing. You can hardly discern good from bad; everything takes on the hue and sheen of goodness.

For Neil and Anita, clocks had stopped ticking and what should have engraved on their heads and minds was the bus driver's twenty minutes. More than one and a half hours had elapsed since they left the bus. Their friends had searched for them but all in vain. There were no tell-tale signs of them and incredible as it would seem no one even grimaced to ask the flowers of the field their whereabouts. It was really disgusting for all when a halo of happiness formed a rainbow in each one of them. Better to feign that these two lovers had booked into some hotel and were busy admiring the works of the Lord, the muscles, the curves and the softness that men and women are made for. Man in every sphere of his life plays with some toy. In childhood, he likes plastic toy cars; when adult he likes big toys, girls above sixteen years and once married chubby, pulsating, lively, smiling real babies whose one glance takes the wear and tear of the day and the incredible stress that knits on your brow to be wiped out by one look of the smiling, knowing, baby face.

The optimists in the bus felt Neil and Anita were nice and snug in some hotel while the pessimists felt Neil or Anita should have informed them about their whereabouts. Were they safe? Shouldn't they wait for them? Hope nothing untoward happened to them. The more the people the more the views. Everybody was in their seat as the bus honked and was off, almost one and a half hours late from the scheduled departure timing.

When it dawned on Anita and Neil who were in a reverie and oblivious of the fact that the bus would be only too happy to travel light without them while the occupants of the bus would still worry about them, it was too late. Soon dusk would be falling and Anita was slightly petrified in this unknown land. Neil tried to make enquiries about transport and found it best to book into a hotel for the night.

Heaven on Earth

Both were taut with excitement by the very thought that they would be together with no one to disturb their love talk. They had conveniently forgotten that walls have ears. Possibly they would pull the ears like a teacher would do to the small kids. Sometimes, doesn't it pay not to be too much cautious? Let life drift its own way and certainly it would frame a very rosy, fulfilling picture for you as it did today. The bus went without them but it was the greatest pleasure a man and woman can have to lovingly hold each other's hands and talk away till the wee hours of the morning. God from Heaven had bequeathed paradise to this lovely loving couple. Which man or which woman would ask for more? A tremor of excitement would run through their body as one skin would not clandestinely but openly touch and feel each other. The temperatures would certainly soar but not one that would burn. It would only give warmth and soothe each other. Neil would be clasping and squeezing her fingers which would annihilate all the blood till it turned whiter but Anita would keep Neil mesmerized with her soft silken tone where they would build their nest, a lovely snug house where she would dote on him and he would be such a caring husband that all her whims and fancies would be attended to lovingly. The air around them would burst out laughing but the inhaled oxygen of the air would choke the exhaled carbon-di-oxide in the nostril from laughing at the preposterous promises being shared by the couple. It had been in and out (inhale, exhale) of so many couples for thousands of years that it knew the inside story of each one of them by heart. The weird promises turn more sensible as days progress and children sprout out from the seeds sown. Both hardly slept for they were busy kissing and squeezing each other. Had this happened in any other country, especially in days gone by, the predicament of the pouting lips of Anita's would have precariously met the father's south paw punch and all her pristine glory would have been the talk of the town. No one can stop wagging tongues and gossip is our favourite pass-time without which life would be very dull, monotonous and insipid. For an average Indian, life narrows down to how many children? Have you got a job? What's cooking today? If you peep into the chatty, (Utensil) you'll find a very watery dal (pulses) with thick chapattis (Bread). If so much is available every day, they would be the happiest in the world. My heart aches to see the sight and plight of the poor. If the well-to-do adopt one-one family and teach them to fish instead of feeding them fish, we'll see more smiling faces amongst us. The rich are extremely rich and the poor, very poor. Forgive me, for taking you away and showing you another world.

The love Neil had for Anita grew stronger as she lay next to him unfolding her dreams to him. He wallowed in every word she uttered like a child hearing the mother's voice. The wisps of her unkempt hair fluttered lazily as his heavy breath kissed the curls, trying to straighten them into submission. The urbane look of Anita had taken its vendetta and she was on the verge of looking a naughty urchin. Neil's thoughts were far off and yet very much with Anita. He was thinking of Anita thirty years from now, when she would be his lawful, doting wife with children big enough to bring in their girl-friends. Where were his thoughts straying? He shook himself from his reverie. Was this called the vicissitudes of life or was he uxorious, a word he had just learnt lately from his friends who were teasing him for he had become extremely fond of Anita and treated her like his inseparable wife.

The hotel or was it a motel for motorists was a nice, clean, snug place unlike the Australian's Worley (a native's hut) or even the African Kraal or the ice-packed Greenland's Eskimos' Igloo. The best part of the room was something soft and warm constantly feeling Neil. It was Anita; what more could he want in life. There was a soft knock on the door for dinner had arrived. Both ate the sumptuous meal without realizing what they gulped; better things were at hand. The chicken-corn soup which normally enters the mischievious, kissable mouths with such a slurping noise was quietly gurgling it's way into the deep confines and dungeons of the stomach like a river in spate after an incessant rain has lashed it's fury. Is it the chicken in the soup which pecks at the corn that initiates the look-down-upon slurping noise. The chicken-corn soup gave it's heat to Neil and Anita's body while the chicken turned cold towards the corn. The unpalatable burping music that follows menacingly after a hearty meal was conspicuous in it's absence showing Anita and Neil coming from well-bred families.

In the morning when they got up, their eyes were full of sleep. They never uttered a good-morning, bonjour (French) nor had they wished each other good-night or their familiar German gute nacht before sleep caught them. All they did now was got entangled in each other's arms and fell off to sleep once again.

Anita dreamt she was in the prairies, the grass-lands of America where the cow-boys ruled and surprisingly Neil also had a dream. He was in the Savannas of Africa where the mighty lions roared but he couldn't be bothered about them for he was cuddled up with Anita and there was no space left in his head, for it was full to the brim with the thoughts of her.

When they rubbed their eyes again to peel off any sleep that was left, they found it was quite late in the evening. Hurriedly they dressed up, hoping to catch their bus but futility had shown the green flag. Somehow they caught a bus to Strasbourg but lurking in the shadows was failure; failure to catch their bus with friends peeping out for them with quizzical and friendly faces.

Enquiry did not reap any harvest but one thing was certain they had to manoeuvre their way to their destination, Berne. Time was already past midnight so they hailed a taxi which screeched to a halt—the concrete stones from the tarred road hurling at the tyres to stop, gives this inimitable screeching sound. They jumped in from the biting cold into the warmth of the heated car—the cold coins and the crispy green currency notes can buy you warmth, eh! Yes, short-lived physical warmth, not the human warmth we look for, which cannot be bought in the open market. Lucky are those who have a lovely home and a wife who is the real hearth of such a home to give this divine heat which warms but does not burn. The cab driver stepped on the gas, it looked the body of the taxi shivered with the cold but the fact remains it was stepped on and with fright and agonizing pain it squealed and then sped away towards Berne.

Love Conquers All

Fortunately Anita remembered the name of the hotel and hoped she wasn't wrong. The right and left lobes of the hemispheres of the brain kept putting different names in the slots allotted as though they were on the game of Sudoku from the newspaper. She harnessed the words on the toilet she had used very recently and took respite from it 'Men to the left as usual and women for they are always Right'. Which foolish man would corroborate such thinking coming from a lady who could give him a cold shoulder and a hot berating tongue. The taxi driver tried to warn them about the late hour for it was almost 2 AM but both were preoccupied with the thought of meeting their friends and so it went into the antennae of one ear and out from the other into the thin, cold air. The driver, it seems felt insulted, took his fare and they saw his receding lights diminish in the cold.

Everything seemed quiet except if you could hear the sound of the flakes of the falling snow. 'PAR EXCELLENCE HOTEL' inspite of the shimmering lights seemed life-less. Neil approached, along with Anita, the porch of the hotel and lightly tapped on the door. There was no response; both Anita and Neil exchanged glances of anxiety. Neil tapped harder at the huge, palatial door but there was not the slightest stir inside. It seemed after a tiring day the staff had sold their horses and gone to bed for there was not the slightest neighing sound.

Neil struck harder at the door; the door did not budge nor did the drooping eye-lids of the workers of the hotel so much as flutter their eye-lashes. It seemed if a hornet's nest was stirred nothing would have alarmed the inmates of the hotel. Try hornets once, my dear friends, and see the consequence of pulling stings for the rest of your life. Where was the sentry on duty? Was he also inside the hotel and fast asleep? First time it dawned on them the taxi-driver was trying to say something but his speech had disappeared in the wilderness of the solitary night. What were they to do now? It was way back after Hitler's regime had reconciled to the way the U.N.O. (United Nations Organisation) would think today and there were no mobiles which have revolutionized the world and one click of it would have brought the world to them. Right now they were clueless and only banged the door. Anita's thoughts veered to her mother in India. She shied away from her mother for unknown to her she was alone with Neil. Strangers know of the deeds of the couple, neighbours come to know soon and poor parents are the last to know the MIS-deeds of their innocent darlings. Now, don't pull my leg—OK, ok, I was also in the same boat when young. So nice, our parents are so inundated in our love. She turned to God and beseeched for his mercy. She felt colder than ever and slowly moved into Neil's ever waiting arms and snuggled to him. Her teeth were chattering and Neil quickly pulled off his coat and covered her with it. She still shivered with the biting cold and thought of the Russian story of 'The Poor Match-Girl' who struck match after match on the phosphorus box to get some warmth but alas; the principles of physics pervaded (Heat lost is equal to heat gained) and so her body absorbed all the cold and she was an ice-statue by morning. Did the same fate await both of them? Who can fight nature and especially when it was wreaking havoc with its icy tentacles. Sleep had gone wool-gathering or was it grazing in the fields and now the pupils of their eyes had dilated with alarm. They moved closer and clung tighter to each other. Each hand tried to pull each other's body in a vice-like grip. The whistling icy wind had subdued to a gentle breeze, so it seemed when two hearts were in embrace. The tighter he squeezed her, the lesser chance of the biting cold to come between them. The icy winds did try to squander some time on these two lovers but their persistence to keep each other warm and safe kept the tantalizing cold away from them. 'Alone I can do nothing but together we can raise hell' and hell is a hot lava of heat from the magma of the sins of the Earth. What a find! A geography teacher will explain better. They were two, Neil and Anita, unlike the Match-Girl who was alone and who had turned into a statue of ice by morning. Alone, Anita had only thought of dying in the cold but together with Neil they had raised all the heat of hell.

The darkness of the night lighted up when dawn announced day-break with their incorrigible silence but persistent trumpets and the mouth of the door of the hotel opened like a savior.

It was loves first victory over cruel nature and perhaps Hitler's Nazis. It was certainly a miracle to be saved from the jaws of icy death. Love defied certain death from the freezing cold of the Alps and sent it scurrying away from its intimidating and harrowing experience of the night.

People in their cozy hotel rooms could feel and see and see the biting cold but could never perceive the certain death that awaited in the shadows of the falling snow-flakes of the night. The sheath of love had annihilated death and sent it sprawling out of the porch of the hotel with its face red out of shame.

The Luscious Lady—India

One-half of our Mother Earth slept, for this part of the hemisphere was plunged in darkness while the other half was bathed in sunlight. The places close to the equator with scorching heat curls the hair of the Africans. Imagine the rays of the Sun 93 million miles away reaching in around 7-8 minutes to the Earth and creating the most mystifying thing in the world—LIFE.

Human life survives the onslaught of every calamity if their body temperature remains 98.4 degrees Fahrenheit. If this body temperature veers up or down, whatever be the reason, it is an usherer for some disease to kick the bucket. Why am I drifting to death when life is just blooming. 'Blooming Idiot 'yes, yes that's just right.

The army trucks still roared past raising all the dust in their fury; the horses of the cavalry still galloped and the infantry soldiers still marched on. Isn't nature's fury like tsunami, earth-quakes, volcanoes, whirl-winds enough that man has to invent man-made devices for his own destruction?

The coffee was in the percolator but trouble was brewing on the home-front—Undivided India. Mahatma Gandhi's stature grew bigger than the biggest statue they could reconcile his image with. With his frugal clothes as he strode from one state and marched to the next, the mighty, invincible British Empire hobbled, limped, slouched to take urgent strides to toy with his colossal idea of leaving India without a fight. The British waddled through with uneasy steps, paced through the corridors of thinking, strolled through the gardens with a heavy heart of leaving 'this luscious lady with a sari' called India. Alternatives they found none and were forced to walk away, back to the British Isles only leaving their imprint on the lives of the Indian people which till today we can't shake off or erase. Bed-tea is a legacy the British left for us. It is more like gargling our mouth with this BAD tea and taking in the night-before bacteria along into the 'sink' of our mouth.

The boom of the canons had ceased and sporadically if it flexed its muscles, the roar of it turned to a whimper and whine of a dog.

Both Anita and Neil had submitted forms for further studies in Germany, but the dormant volcano of action by the Indians suddenly spurt into gear what had been idling for years together. Neil decided to rush to India to his family along with Anita but she also wanted to see her family. Two tickets were booked to Delhi by Lufthansa Airways but last minute Anita changed her flight to Lahore much to the latent chagrin of Neil which he sealed inside his lips and did not utter a word, he simply adored Anita to speak anything against her. How he wished she would change her plans and come with him to Delhi and from there he would accompany her to Lahore which was an over-night journey by the steam-engine (train). The coal-ash that flew anointed most of the passengers close to the engine, free of cost and got into their eyes to gauge their suffering of discomfort. Unlike the potato, Neil was of a very cool temperament, like a cucumber difficult to change even in very trying times. A potato just boiled is normally refused entry in the mouth by the very discerning tongue. Add a little salt and pepper to the mashed potato, make little flattened balls with it and fry it brown with a little olive oil, add a dash of tamarind chutney and a little yoghurt and lo and behold, the spoon won't get a chance to rest for the tongue would be lolling out of the mouth for more and yet more. ("Do patte tikki" to the chaatwala—two plates of chaat). Be careful the north (tongue) and the south (the bottom) of a man are always at war and ready to show a man down by making him run to the wash-room for refuge. Potatoes, as ugly as they look with stretch-marks of the good earth all over them, when mixed with brinjals for the vegetarians and mutton for the non-vegetarians leaves such a relishing, languishing taste in the mouth that you don't wish to spoil it by gulping anything after it. Long live the taste, long live the potato. A child above four-five years can be trusted to tell the truth whether the food served is good or not. His taste-buds have not changed tracks as do the teens and above who like even the taste of the bitter liquor. Worth watching their taut faces as they gulp their peg, is reminiscent of someone forced to take poison. The potato when blended with methi (fenugreek) is a realm of just a few who take it more for it's medicinal property. Some are bound to disagree here but my idea of the savoury and unsavoury potato is to mix and make friends with the right people who will make you even better than what you are. Do good and bask in it's aroma and see the happiness that descends on you. War will be a thing of the past and no shades of it will ever touch humanity.

Anita's people were equally anxious to see and meet Neil for Anita had made it amply clear that there would be no one else except Neil in her life. From the description she had given in three dimensions (3 D) about him, anyone would loathe to hear anything bad about him. He may not be prince Toolu but certainly a prince in his own dimension. Truly he was able to carry that portrait of a charming prince to the hilt. He was a true gentleman where his character was concerned and soft-spoken and yet full of fun. He was already welcome like a lord and master in Anita's house. The initial frown that had grown on the trunk of this house-hold looked ugly and out of place and vanished like the horns of a donkey to be replaced by succulent and luscious faces that loved to be licked and kissed. Was Anita good in portraying Neil's image or was it the true love that sauntered to break all boundaries and carve a niche for themselves. Eyes were full of dreams and dreams had broken its shackles and were floating all around. Every two steps these two lovers saw rosy dreams; dreams that would soon materialize into 'Pinch and See' the truth; dreams that carried a halo of a rainbow around it. What consternation, what surprises were in store for the most satisfying, rejuvenated couple of the century.

Everyone talks of a storm in a tea-cup but here in India trouble was brewing since the British announced India's shackles of slavery would be removed and Freedom given at the stroke of mid-night of 15th of August 1947. The gust of wind of disgust did blow, religion which teaches patience and love for mankind had taken on the hue of an ogre in disguise and turned full India into a slaughter-house. See the irony of man, there are rules governing cruelty to animals inside this very loathsome house, more so for a vegetarian. Yet no rules adorn any walls where specialization in cruelty to man is concerned. The worse, the better applauded, like peeling the skin of a live man and the raw flesh draws squeaks and laughter from the perpetrators. Man has two sides to his nature, the wild and cruel and the other loving and forgiving. One religion was fighting another creating a rift between man and man and causing untold misery in this civil war of butchering one another.

It's the huge mass of water that separated the enormous land mass which was one big chunk but now separated into continents and countries because the shallow land was gulped by the seas and oceans. Before the Pacific Ocean, the Arctic Ocean, the Indian Ocean came into existence, the earth called PANGAEA, was one piece of land. There would have been no fighting for your country and no boundaries. No standing in queues for passports and visas and hopefully, no blood-shed.

Every now and then the very gruesome things of life take me away and my deer readers, yes the doe-eyed ones and the very muscular from the central characters. Neil who had reached Delhi and Anita who had reached Lahore, was a Bastian of majority of the people and the latter that of the minorities.

Neighbours, whether they belonged to the majority or the minorities, had a very peaceful co-existence. Holi, Eid, Diwali, the colourful festivals would only enhance the love between the two and bring them closer in a cohesive society. Eagles-eyes of the opportunist goondas and villains would always look to create trouble between the two. Slightest veneer that looked bruised would be utilized to plunge the two into fighting. Illiterate as these loafers, villains are but shrewdness to capitalize at the right moment is their utmost joy and forte-in so doing, they benefit from the chaos. Why doesn't the good Earth on which these hooligans stand become quick-sand to swallow them in? I always wonder and my mind wanders how such a handful of these unscrupulous, illiterate people can sway the masses and create ripples and hysteria that people are scared of their own shadows, leave alone neighbours and strangers. Besides the gossip, neighbours always, anywhere in the world, live in harmony giving security unawares to each other. And strangers why should they harm us when we have not harmed them. Yes, insecurity of our lives makes us give the first blow even when the stranger is harmless. This frenzy and hysteria of insecurity is the brain-child of these muscle-men who thrive creating such a macabre thinking amongst us to pilfer other people's life-savings. Mankind beware of such life-sucking parasites, who hide behind the writings of religions, misconstrue words or play with the sentiments of people to incite one against the other. This venom, this poison should be extracted, as scientists do from poisonous snakes to create anti-serum to annul the effects of the snake-bite. Doesn't the majority of the people live my dream of converting the world into a fairy-land of love and sheer happiness. To be Good in all circumstances should be the religion of the people—and then see the world sway from chaos and misery to one of life's fulfillment and to be on Cloud Nine of Happiness. Those who watched the killings especially wives and daughters were horrified and just sank seeing their men-folk meted out with such horrible deaths. Worse was when the men had to watch their wives and daughters being degraded. My hand shivers and shakes to hear of such indignities to women and refuses to put pen to paper for everything and anything would turn crimson with shame, seeing the most debasing things being done in the orgy and frenzy of partition. Derision would make people vomit, commit suicide or even kill the perpetrators. It was a scene even hard hearted soldiers would avoid and prefer a full throated war than this concept of a civil war. Shots of the gun ring out, canons boom and the enemy just collapses. This is a soldier's life but he gets no thrill and refrains from ever torturing or peeling the skin of a live man and seeing the agony in his eyes or the slow crawling of death.

Pages of history were being filled and the scenario of the geography of the country that the British were chewing succulently for almost two hundred years was divided into Pakistan and India.

All the villains, goondas, vagabonds, muscle-men with cruel intentions came out in crowds all over India especially the Wagah and Attari Borders and massacred as many people to loot them who were fleeing the country. Same was the case on the other side of the fence where they singled out people, slit their throats and took away all their belongings.

The same hand which can cushion a child was thwarted and used in this menacingly inhuman way. Was it all the human A B C—were in disarray and needed proper sorting so that humanity could click back into its slots? Any normal person would fail to understand the blood-bath. You want to go to Pakistan, you go. I want to stay in India, I stay. Was it the handiwork of unscrupulous persons who had become rich overnight for it was witnessed people searching the pockets of the dead and the dying. Necklaces, ear-rings, nose-studs and their life-savings which they carried in a piece of cloth clutched tightly in their hands or deep-down in their vest pockets and above all the precious, yellow metal hidden in the ladies' petticoats was just pulled out as would a tiger springing on a deer for the kill. Those who watched felt nauseated. Is it the good Earth that needs blood every now and then to satiate it's hunger. This is something which is visible in every part of the world. More than a million Jews had just been able to quench Hitler's thirst for blood, in the form of revenge till he lay dying at St. Helena much exasperated and disgusted with life. Take the case of Hiroshima and Nagasaki in Japan. The United Nations Combined Forces had to flex their muscles in Sudan and Afghanistan etc to cow down the uprisings and yet blood kept flowing.

Wet Trousers

The atmosphere was tense with bullets straying away from the actual targets. It was a civil war and people who had never held the cold steel of a gun were pressing the trigger more with fright than to keep the enemy at bay.

I would like to steal the thunder right from under my lovely reader's feet to soothe their nerves by taking them away and showing in a lighter vein some embarrassing moments of my life. I can see mouth-watering eagerness to read this.

Doing a short term entrepreneurial management course at Lucknow with experts from the faculty of small industries, the very first lecture was from a psychologist. He swayed us with his carefully selected words, as would a snake-charmer a snake, with his musical flute. With the velvety flow of words, all the boys' limbs twitched, the palms of the hands itched to start working. It would take a long time for the professor to come down from his rostrum. For want of time, we would hurriedly visit a market twenty minutes away and have fruit-chaat for lunch (fruit-salad). First two days I enjoyed the freshly cut delectable fruit chaat with lemon juice squeezed on top.

It was the third day as far as I remember. Normally the fruit in the chaat would go down titillating the esophagus and sit down quietly in the stomach for its turn to mix with the digestive juices to go down further. It did not happen this time. The fork pierced the heart of the banana piece in the plate. As soon as the banana, pine-apple, orange, apple pieces were ruthlessly pushed into the cave of the mouth, the jaw gnashed its teeth and like a pneumatic hammer set to work and converted everything to pulp. Seething with rage at the disgrace the fruits were meted out with, the minced fruits held a flag meeting to take revenge. The decision was unanimous to exit from the body at the earliest.

I heard a growling sound inside my stomach as though all the drains in the world had found an opening and unleashing their fury of dirt. I told my friends to go for classes while I would take a little time to come as I had some work but did not tell the actual reason out of shame.

My legs and thighs were entwined for fear something slimy might ooze out and wet my pants. There was another growl and then everything was quite quiet on the war front.

For fear no one was watching, I trotted the road not that I could gallop. I wish I had a mirror to see the look on my face. It must have been miserable but all my friends who are eyeing me for a wet patch on my pants must have certainly gone through this agonizing retreat somewhere in life, so don't give that convincing x-Ray, know-all smile.

In this unknown market where was I to find a bath-room. In the time I asked, the flood-gates of the back-door might open and the stigma attached to it loomed worse than leprosy. I asked two shop-keepers and both pointed towards the far end. The clocks were ticking and every second counted for the deluge could arrive in a split second.

I discarded every thought that was trying to ease me and took on to trespass anybody's house and walk into their bathroom without permission, such was the urge. 'Trespassers would be prosecuted 'had no numbing effect on me. I would just walk into the first house I came across.

There was a flight of steps and how I covered it, is anybody's guess. I pushed a big glass gate, saw a man standing and asked him I wanted to use the wash-room. He must have seen the distorted look on my face and pointed to a room. It could not have been the forty days, forty nights deluge but certainly the fastest one in history and what a relief! I thanked the man and then I saw bottles and tinkling of glasses with ice and tipplers drowning their sorrows in the liquor. It was a bar and the man, the barman. As yet, no one has ever enticed me with a drink and so I do not know the ecstasy it leaves you in. If Shakespeare was alive he would have uttered "Et tu Francis" if he had found me in the bar. No amount of persuasion would have made anyone believe why I was in the bar.

How I reconnoitered those kissable steps, which took the urge off me, I perceive the Ethiopian Olympic runners could not have beaten me. I had hardly crossed the last step when the urge was back with a vengeance. I clasped my thighs and my legs together as would 'Poison Ivy', a creeper, curl itself onto a tree.

How I dragged myself up the vicious steps now, in this unsightly, ungainly position I leave it to you to visualize and have that twinkle in your eyes. One man's pain is another man's delight.

The ascent of Everest by Edmond Hillary and Tenzing Norgay to climb 29,028 feet must not have been so treacherous as were these steps.

Surprise writ large on the barman's face he uttered "You just—" but I had vanished into the washing room without hearing him. After the guttural smile had made inroads onto my smooth face with wrinkles, I sang out "What a relief"!

Long afterwards shuttling between the valley of tears and smiles, I suggested to myself loud and clear "Everything else in this world can wait but not so a child and loose motions".

Where to Hide My Face

We are on the road to embarrassment. The tyres are screeching and the brakes have failed. Who will then, stop me from narrating this episode. All these years it was a captive, huddled behind a constipated stern look.

I'm principal of a school where we shower our meagre benevolence on the not-so-privileged. My three children lovingly call me 'Crazy' and their friends call me 'The only satisfied man in the world.'

We have a staff-room where teachers in their free period sit and do corrections and gossip, the favourite past-time of all, more ladies than men. Straight from the staff-room, runs a flight of fourteen steps leading to other class-rooms. During recess, before the school starts and after school one teacher on top of the steps, one teacher on the ground floor and a worker at a very strategic position in the middle of the steps are stationed to avoid any mishap of children slipping and falling down.

It has been smooth sailing all along in the 38 years of the school, till I unabashedly came Para-gliding down the steps. There was nothing very extra-ordinary for a principal to slip, after all he is just as human as anybody else. He knows Newton's laws of gravity, frictional forces etc. like anybody else and everybody after a hearty laugh at his fall and 'Why didn't he break his neck'? would have hushed up and subsided.

How would you react if you were told that the principal after his roller-coaster ride down the steps landed on the ground where the children had gathered for him. Teachers and some big boys and girls rushed to pull him up from the ground where he was licking the dust. Nice taste, eh! I could not see my own face, I sure must have blushed with streaks of embarrassment showing all over my pink cheeks.

I wish to forget such incidences but the thoughts corner me with ugly faces of delight.

Save Me from this Embarrasing Inferno

Political parties I just detest but this was someone I could not just shake off. He was very close to my heart and I wanted him to win. One call and he would come running to help. Be it the scorching heat of a summer afternoon, when the mercury with its relentless energy from the sun would dance it's way like a snake to 45 degrees centigrade, but this person would come running with eyes half closed with sleep. The proverbial forty winks had not finished it's count and he was there at my beck and call. On a cold frosty night, he would leave a warm inviting bed to attend to my summons. For the first time in his life he had opened his mouth to invite me and I would shudder to even think of saying "No".

I refused to sit on the dias with some eminent politicians of this place and sat with the masses, many of whom turned out to be parents of my school children, past and present. I was regaled with a lot of namastes (good-afternoon etc.) handshakes as I sat amidst them.

It was touching to get so much respect from so many. People on my left, people on my right didn't miss the opportunity to shake hands with me. People in front drew my attention with their waving hands. Gingerly I stole a look at the back and saw eyes and hands trying to draw my attention. Surely as a financial benefactor to many of them for the last 38 years had yielded such a harvest of love and then I was caught in the quagmire of words of the speaker and got lost in him.

Speaker after speaker kept pouring in elucidating the fact that the political candidate and my trust-worthy friend was the only correct choice to put the ballot for. Almost 45 minutes to one hour may have past when I got up from the reverie of their intoxicating words.

I looked left, I looked right, I looked front, I looked back but the huge wave and multitude of people almost pushing each other in these chairs had simply vanished.

The crowd had not dwindled but the tsunami of heads had receded away from me as though I was a leper and coming close would only invite the dreadful disease.

I put my harness of thoughts and let my imagination run wild. One minute the people were all mine and I felt awed at the love they showered on me and the next minute they had shriveled into their cocoons after paying their respects to me. What I forgot that the people were only doing their duty and moving away from me. There was no love-loss for them. They had taught me the difference between love and paying your respects.

I consoled myself, perhaps, lack of words or communication skills had kept the swarm of well-wishers away from me but to think that in such a huge crowd you are the only isolated person and no one in the vicinity of your left, right, front and back makes you believe you are from the zoo. People see and move on, good way of thanks-giving.

I introspect and a flood of thoughts drenches me right up to the left and right hemispheres of my brain and shakes these two dormant lobes into activity.

Such a small fry like me feels the insinuation of insults then, I wonder, what big benefactors go through.

Drinks and The Devil Go Hand In Hand

Not in the blistering, scorching heat of May, June when the mercury rushes up to take in fresh, cool breeze as we do going up the hills but in the freezing cold of January my sister and her husband decided to get their daughter married. Society has done a commendable job by introducing the institution of marriage. No loafers, vagabonds can just force and walk away with your daughter legally unless she spurns your hand and holds his entwining fingers. Marry and be merry in a hurry and repent at leisure. It seems love emanates from a magnet in the heart which is weak for the road-side Romeos and very strong for the one man one woman love who stick together for eternity. The other theory of love maybe these muscle-men get temporary magnetism of love with electricity after all the human body is made up of elemental iron, calcium, magnesium etc., etc. and deficiency of one leads to anaemia etc. The stick-fast husband and wife are those with permanent magnets which cannot be switched off. The other more plausible theory is a girl happily and willingly leaving her home, as did her mother years back, to become the lady and the boss of the house with her hot, scalding tongue. How often we have heard the oft quoted words from the husband 'I'm the boss of this house and I have got permission from my wife to say so'.

Marriage time is fun time. It was more exciting since we arranged everything for the wedding. The tedious job of distribution of cards to the guests was their own responsibility. Rest of the work was left in our warm laps and we did not wait for it to hatch out. Everything was very synchronized. The pandals (Tents) were put, the stage set for the bride and bride-groom to sit and the caterers were put on the job to serve a delectable dinner. They did a commendable job, as they always do, and everyone got busy munching and crunching.

Normally, the bride-groom arrives much in advance and waits for his bride to arrive in church for the nuptial ceremony. In this case the bride was brought to the church on time while the bride-groom was still trying to hide the blemishes on his face with some lotions and creams, so it seemed. The clock whirred and struck the 5o'clock appeal for the bride-groom to show his chivalrous face. He arrived almost half-an-hour late when all the guest's patience had run out and much to the chagrin of the parish priest who was to solemnize the marriage. Even the hands of the clock in the church moved lazily and lethargically as though it had no other work but then have you heard of clocks doing any other work except keeping people on their toes? You are running late and today your boss will blast you and perhaps show you the door with a blue ticket. It sees the good time and the harrowing time of all the people in its vicinity. It puffs up in happiness with its gong singing away in joyous melody and sometimes silently suffers the depression of its owners. Sadly in a melancholy voice it announces your time is up and you are ready to kick the bucket. Marriage time is no time to reconcile your happy moments with misery.

The organ and the choir lustily drowned all such thoughts as the bride-groom slipped his arm into the bride's arm and led her up the aisle. A man is the happiest on the day of his marriage and unawares gives away his freedom in this web of matrimony. He is like a pre-nursery child wanting to go to school without knowing what he is delving into.

It was nice and warm inside the church with most of the doors shut. Only the entrance door was open and the one next to it, ajar.

With 300-400 guests breathing out hot carbon-di-oxide in the church, it was manageable for the bride-groom's side to feel cozy and wanted.

The rings had been exchanged, the witnesses had decorated their signatures in the marriage register and the priest had acknowledged their 'I do 'with his blessings. The veil of the bride was lifted and the first kiss planted on his brand new wife by the husband. Now what is planted and if watered and cared for must bear flowers and fruits and it did as time progressed.

Everyone was out of the church and into the biting cold. Suddenly there was a rush of people like the Gold Rush of Johannesburg of South Africa. There was a circle of people holding the mother-in-law of the bride. She was shivering violently and her teeth were chattering. Monkey's chatter—was she turning into a monkey? This was no time to fool around. Coming from south of India she could not bear the cold of the north (of India). Quickly we pushed her into a car and put the car heater on full. Finding her still shivering and quivering we rushed her to her hotel room.

Some gossip-mongers whispered in a hushed tone that she could collapse, so my wife sent me to get rum that she would rub under her feet to get warmth and maybe give her a little to drink for heat.

I stood in line to buy a rum bottle in a wine-shop. Standing next to me was one school parent who held me in high esteem for not touching the bottle and would quote me as an example to his friends.

He saw me and I turned pale and when he uttered "You also started drinking sir", I turned cold.

Did You Hear that Rustling Noise or See that White Figure?

We have an unlikely huge dining table, infact two big tables put together, to seat almost 15-20 people comfortably at one time. Cosy feelings, eh? Not so, not in the least especially in winters.

A cold, spine chilling breeze saunters its way from the ventilators and the windows of the first floor. How stealthily the cold creeps in and wraps like mufflers around the ones seated for break-fast. They would not only be served omelet, toast, cheese, parantha but for the dessert, pneumonia.

All of us would shirk the dining table in winters and seek the warmth and refuge of the kitchen where our mother would regale us with stories. Eight of us would be huddled over a soft-coke fire on wooden stools and small iron chairs. Occasionally, if it was dinner time my closest friend, Sudhir Chowdhry, would join us. I don't wish to get into that nostalgic fever for fear of meningitis (fever—Ha, Ha.).

My mother who was very fond of reading would unfold stories after stories of spirits and ghosts. Putting a bold front, when actually we shivered and shook from inside, we would ask her for more.

There was an empty house not far from where my parents lived. Everyone in the vicinity said it was haunted.

Doing the rounds was that an English gentleman who was killed on the Mall Road, still walked the road reading a newspaper. Anyone who wished him "Good Morning" while passing would get a reply back. The newspaper would come down from the reading position and what the wisher would see was a European with no head. (eeeeee . . . .)

At the stroke of midnight, the tick-tock of the clocks may not be audible but those of dancing girls, in this haunted house, with ghungroos (small bells on the Indian dancer's feet) could be heard clearly. Everyone believed spirits were responsible for this.

With this story of ghungroos in mind we children slept off. Six lovely brothers, sisters dreamt of chocolate houses and had a peaceful sleep.

It was the urge of nature at 2 am which tip-toed and whispered in my ears to get that 'what a relief' feeling.

Not to disturb anyone, I quietly slipped off the bed to the drain in our house to relieve myself.

I had hardly started when last night's ghungroos (bells) rang out. You may have heard of people wetting their pants in fright. Mine stopped flowing but in that split-second I realized it was Sadul's (neighbour) horse with bells on his neck that it shook and dried up my blood.

A Wonderful Human Being

In Lahore (now Pakistan), to be specific, lived a happy family with assets that a normal house-hold would be proud of. The man was Iqbal Khan and his wife, Rehana and three children stayed together least suspecting that a tsunami of hatred would destroy and sink their indestructible, invincible Titanic home. Iqbal Khan was every inch a European who had studied in Oxford University in London. He smoked Cuban cigars, wore a solar hat and a suit and tie to match. He had borrowed every facet of their lives and had a heart of gold.

On either side of Iqbal's house lived two families, one Mr. Bhattacharya, a Bengali and the other from north India. They would tease Iqbal that he had just one strand of hair sprouting out of his bald head (Ek-Baal) and all three would laugh contagiously. (Iq-one, bal-hair)

As waves of violence incinerated, both these families sent their wives and children to safety while they stayed on for the deluge of anger and mistrust to abate. The anger, mistrust and hatred rose and fell like the high and low tide of the oceans and seas. Tempers would cool down they thought and soon they would bring their families back. They were surrounded from all sides by lovely loving families who treated them with a lot of love and respect. Special sevayya (vermicelli) would arrive at the door-step of Bhattacharya and Devinder Singh on Eid. (Muslim festival)

Now came the litmus test if their love in a different atmosphere survived. Faces that were strewn with buds of smiles and laughter opened up like thorny cactus at the mere sight of the minorities at that particular juncture. Overnight, it seemed, ugly warts had surreptitiously crept on the faces with discernable hatred and fear of each other.

On both sides of the Borders of the partitioned countries, India and Pakistan, blood was splattering as though humans were like chickens and fit for the slaughter. Attari and Wagah borders were scenes of most gruesome, heinous and sadistic pleasures of a different kind—blood-curdling killing in the name of God.

When the sight of the red gurgling blood over-flowed in the drains and nallahs, the blood-thirsty drank in its Heavenly bliss and the weak at heart fainted unable to see the ire, the wrath turning the colour surrounding the retina into a frenzy of white. How dreadful! Did the 'CREATOR' in HIS wildest imagination ever think such death awaited HIS play-toys (Humans). If the two hands and tongue had worked to stop the killings it would have done more than a full Nation's hands clasped in prayer. Writers keep warning all and sundry but all their efforts fall on deaf ears. God, knowingly, so sweetly created two ears, one for hearing and the other one to let it out. Loquacious tongues spit fire for one community to get against the other. Religions that soothed the nerves were stirring a tsunami without inhibition and laughter would gurgle out seeing the maimed and the slaughtered. Love, like air, which is free would be detested and a weapon of the weak. Inimical rivalry without inordinate delay, would be the two arch enemies to succumb to. Arms and hands that had nurtured the babies were simply used like robots without feelings to twist the necks. Blood had possibly congealed on their eyes for they could not see or perceive and a cloud of religious aura had kept them numb and bereft of human feelings and emotions.

Cauldrons of hot lava of anger and inimical feelings had filled the drains to the brim when eyes turned to the neighbours. Someone sneaked and both Devinder Singh and Bhattacharya were drumming on the doors of Iqbal Khan with a strain of anxiety to open the door fast. Both flung at the feet of Iqbal to hide them from the nefarious knives of the tormentors. Anxiety, trepidation and fear writ large on Iqbal Khan's face, he ushered them closer and whispered to hide on the terrace which had no steps running to it but a ladder would suffice in the dark. Mr.

Iqbal could just walk out of the house and give away the hide-out of his neighbours to the seekers to save his own skin, so precious is one's own life that anybody else would have run from the noose. Not so Iqbal, who was full of compassion and would take the risk even if he died saving the two. Countries should be secular not just by name but by their deeds and war of any kind should be banned with UNO taking the lead to stop, along with the help of world leaders. Show the brutalities of wars and world wars to the general public so that wives curb their husband's tendencies towards their brutal nature. The idea of teaching History is to abstain from wars and not learn new tactics to fight. Turn a deaf ear but be sure someone is crying somewhere instead of laughing. I just hope it is not someone close to you when you will feel the pain and the significance of war. Readers, most probably, will omit reading this—I can only offer my apologies.

Back to the facts of our story—In the darkness of the night a rope would be pulled up at the end of which would be a basket filled with chapaties (Indian bread) and vegetables plus a utensil filled with water. This would go up and their hunger and thirst would go down, quenched and satiated. From the inferno of the afternoon which would even dry up the marrow of the bones, the muscles and every pore of the skin would cry out for water and more water. Both Bhattacharya and Devinder Singh would lie flat on the roof in the sweltering heat of a Pakistani summer. The thermometer itself getting blisters from the rising temperature of 45 degrees centigrade (113 degrees Fahrenheit). Any movement on the terrace would reveal their hide-out by the neighbours. Silently, both would pray that they don't become a prey to any passing helicopter or an aeroplane. Two days and two nights of anguish and vigil gave birth to a brilliant idea. People had been knocking on the door of Iqbal and asking about Devinder and Bhattacharya's where-abouts and Iqbal Khan would show ignorance while his heart-beat would put a running leopard's heart-beat to shame.

Iqbal dressed Bhattacharya in his own clothes. Tie to match, a Cuban cigar in his mouth and a solar hat adorning his head. He just walked out and disappeared in the crowd.

It was a scene enacted straight from a Hollywood or Bollywood cinema, maybe a James Bond movie.

Next was Devinder Singh's chance. Dressed to the hilt like Iqbal Khan, a thick Burma cheroot (cigar) in his mouth with smoke billowing out in circles and the coveted solar hat effacing all of Devinder Singh and bringing in a new Iqbal. Out of the gate walked he, with some neighbours even wishing him. He just shook his head and trotted on. His heart was pounding like an over-worked machine. He told his face not to betray him at this crucial hour. He begged of his many Gods not to forsake him and made promises of feeding a hundred beggars if he came out unscathed from their clutches into the safe newly formed Indian Territory.

Just imagine an exodus of 7,000,000 (approx seven million) minorities from India to Pakistan and 6,000,000 (approx Six million) outsiders fleeing from Pakistan to India. I'm trying to emphasize the figures to show the magnitude and seriousness of the occasion. You could draw a parallel with the wildebeest in Africa crossing the river Mara and the crocodiles waiting with their open jaws in the water.

One person is killed and the blood that pours causes nausea amongst us. One million should cause hatred for wars and civil wars. The ladies especially have a big hand in stopping their husband and brothers from war. Peace would reign like incessant rain. Just give it a thought and a try.

Devinder Singh had passed all hurdles and was almost past the Wagah Border when someone knowing spotted him and asked him to remove his solar hat. Already a crowd had formed around him and all had started pushing and pulling him in their uncouth ways. His solar hat went flying. His tie was used as a lasso, as they do to catch horses, to push and pull him. The buttons of his shirt could not stand their scrutiny and one by one gave up. In a crowd no one shows a gentlemanly behaviour. They behave what they actually are in real life—niggers. You will never find a real gentleman in the midst of such hooligans—he will quietly take the narrow lane home.

They wanted to catch the person who gave him sanctuary for so long and put his own neck in trouble. The Good Earth on which he stood shivered and shook that it would soon be witness to this brutal killing. How this Earth wished that it's shivering turn into an Earth-Quake of 8.3 on the Richter scale to stop this killing. What it forgot thousands would be buried in the building collapse and debris. It didn't have the IQ of a man. They man-handled him and asked him how he was alive so long. "Where was he hiding?" He had no say of his own; words just fell off his tongue in fright and the last anyone heard from him was Iqbal Khan "Oh! The traitor—we'll fix him", they shouted. From amongst the crowd a lean man just walked away. This was the same man who Iqbal Khan had helped get a job and now he was on his way to inform Iqbal that the crowd was coming to kill him and his family for helping an outsider.

Run Iqbal Run

Iqbal Khan with his family ran for his life to the railway station where a train was just pulling out but had to stop a number of times because of chain pulling. The Wheels reluctantly moved for 15-20 minutes and then stopped. Nobody could ascertain what had happened and there was no one to stand and give a plausible reason and maybe, confront death in a rare case of partition of a country.

The train was jam-packed and over-flowing with humans. Our English teacher would call "packed like sardines". What the world is not aware and what I lisp and feel ashamed to say and what our mother and father felt proud was the 'pride' of children, blessed from above, that they had holed up in a small room, thirteen to the count. The resilience to over-crowding started in our homes where we got acclimatized like sardines and which could be seen now when we accommodated every new entrant to our bogey.

The train refused to budge, more like the dormant Vesuvias volcano of Sicily.

Mr. Iqbal quickly changed the train along with his family. Seeing the children's suffering, a European allowed them into his coupe. Hardly had they made themselves comfortable when their previous stationary train started, with all the coal dust nestling itself in every nostril to trigger an epidemic of asthma later on in life.

Mrs Rehana Khan chided her husband seeing the other train receding in the distance. She was no different from other ladies who love to chew the cud for she kept on reminding him about it as and when an opportunity occurred. The European sat quietly reading some papers and never showed any anxiety about the movement of the train. Either patience was imbrued in him or he had imbibed it from the Indians in his long stay in undivided India. The only thing, I presume, that worried him was the heat and the raging Loo of north India. Very hot, dry winds blow in north India in summer called Loo and temperatures run to 45 degrees centigrade to 50 degrees centigrade. (122 degrees F)

It was almost two hours later when the train showed any signs of life and crawled its way. If anyone wanted to see a picture of anxiety and uneasiness and most of all fear then every face in the train reflected it. People going through the same anguish were scared of the people sitting next to them, sometimes even of their own shadows. Man cannot live in solitary confinement and yet today he could not discriminate Tom, Dick and Harry from his foes for every manoeuvre of theirs was an eerie silence to the horror they would perpetrate at the right opportunity—'let not your left hand know what your right hand is doing'.

The train ran unmindful of the frenzy in the air, did not even choke when it ran over dead bodies on the slippery rails. The iron wheels turned human form into mince-meat and the red of the blood looked like Dracula wearing lipstick for it gloated on every bump it received as it passed over any dead body. These were stray cases of killings.

Nobody was complaining for lips were sealed. Sleep had just vanished, eye-lids were not drooping inspite of 3-4 days of no sleep as though the eye-lashes had lashed the eye with a whip, as would a cop a robber.

The train had snaked its way through green fields and more often barren. It had already meandered through enough kilometers for everyone's eyes to secretly heave a sigh of relief when screeching sound of the brakes broke their reverie

The eyes just popped out of their sockets at the ghastly sight that greeted the images on the screen of their retinas. Bodies and more bodies were strewn all over the place. Gashes, slit throats, life hammered out with sticks and stones, pure knuckle power had done most of the damage as the mangled bodies lay sprawled in their own blood and dust of the earth from which they had sprung up.

The train Iqbal and his family had left was standing right next to their present train. Hoodlums from one particular belief had come like locusts and pulled out innocent people from the train, old, young, middle-aged irrespective of their being male or female and massacred them in cold blood. Families after families were dragged out of the compartments and mercilessly killed. It would not be possible for me to narrate the scenes of the killings for my vocabulary itself would start bleeding and no nurse or doctor would be able to stop the flow. Just for a second think your daughter or your wife or for that matter even your husband were the victims of such degrading, inhuman brutalities wouldn't your head burst or go insane? I believe war must just be stopped on any count and if all the countries unite which country will have the audacity to even wear the harness of war.

Now a scene that unfolds and comes very clear on the human screen of the mind were certain people who looked like parasites and lived and relished on the dead. These few shameless people were moving from body to body and pulling necklaces, bangles, ear-rings, etc of gold and from some dead men with bulging pockets of paper currency. Overnight these beggars had become rich, stinking rich for the smell they carried was that of a grave-yard with nauseating bones all over. Can our society stand such perverts?

The journey that was just over-night took three days and three nights to reach its destination and surprisingly without any further mishap.

Love in Times of War

Delhi and Lahore were on the boil and from the steam more latent heat spouting out at the borders.

True love survives the heat of the day, the coolness of the night, does not get moist with 99 % humidity or even rain of Cherrapunji in Assam, India which has the highest rainfall in the world. Lust will just wither away like a delicate flower, true love will thrive and wallow even in the mire and dirt of the Good Earth. There's a lilt in the cacophony of music that it lucidly plays while lust goes livid and dies an unnatural death.

Day in and day out, how Neil wished Anita was in his arms and she on her part was only thinking of new recipes. She knew the road to a man's heart was over his tongue, if the taste was palatable and delicious there was no escape for him. As yet the gravity of the partition had not sunk in. Whatever she heard from her near and dear ones Anita took it with a pinch of salt. Otherwise also she was a home-bird and did not know the reality of outside or the curtain of love made the outside picture translucent or even opaque at times that she could not perceive what was happening. In true love nothing makes a difference. She felt it was a passing phase and everything would subside and her prince charming, Neil, would come and three banns of marriage would be crooned by the priest from the church's pulpit and she would bathe in happiness.

Thoughts lead to action. Anita was as placid as a calm sea till now. How did the dormant volcano suddenly become active? There's a limit for anyone's patience and when the cup is full and ebbs over, a flutter of hurricane follows. Such characters who are stoically calm unleash an unsubsiding wave of treacherously sinister thought-provoking action. Only a concussion to the head brings them back to their normal self.

There was no news from Neil which made her like a wounded tigress with cubs. Her asthmatic father tried to pacify her to be a little patient for the fury to subside but it did not strike the right chord for her to come to her senses. Love is blind and can make you completely blind. Any entreaties only register on a deaf ear. You know you are doing wrong but you will not whimper slightly in doing so. Such is love and those who have not gone through the pangs of it will find it hard to digest all this unsavoury attitude and will find it difficult to thaw in such perplexed circumstances. Don't we harp that everything is fair in love and war. The situation here was intense love with a burning desire and a petrifying war that was ready to burn and destroy anyone at the whimsical flip of a finger and take delight at the atrocity.

Anita's mother tried to pacify her but this was not platonic love to cool off with prudence and understanding. The more she tried to vociferously prolong her stay the more adamant she became to reach Delhi. Love is blind. How else would inter-caste marriages take place? They do bring a lot of people and relations together inspite of the initial hesitation. Her decision out-weighed all the father, mother's entreaties. Her mother's eyes were so full of the salty-water that small dams had formed in the sockets of her eyes and rivulets of tears streaked down her cheeks forming streams. Father, mother's love which is paramount in anyone's life had fizzled out in front of Neil's love. This is the only philosophy on how a girl leaves her home to make a home for herself as her mother had done and to bring in her off-springs for the world population to expand.

Fire was not just burning in Anita's heart but an inferno had started in Neil's heart who had thrown all caution to the winds and like a mad man was running through Connaught Place of Delhi towards the railway station. All the pleadings of the father and mother were not palatable and that he was a grown-up man ready to take his own decisions. Neil's father reconciled to the fact that in his own life he had taken decisions which his son was doing now. History was repeating itself while Neil's geography was ready to study Anita's (geography).

The pandemonium of the partition of the country into India and Pakistan, which had crippled and maimed many families and wiped out many more from the face of the earth, had not even remotely affected the love of Neil and Anita. Every breath they inhaled and exhaled brought out bubbles of love-lorn faces of both of them.

Only an introvert would have thought of the half empty glass of miseries but Neil being an extrovert only thought of the other half full glass of happiness that awaited him on reaching Lahore. With such conditions prevailing in the country any means of communications was just not possible. Mobile phones were not invented till then or else this problem would have never arisen. Even if the post-office was open chances of telegrams being sent or received were rather slim and which post-man would take the telegram to its addressee unless he was sick of his life and wanted to end it. Neil had, somehow, to reach Lahore, hold Anita in his vice-like grip and pour the love he had for Anita. It was not easy to get a train at that time; if you got one it was so crowded that to get one foot in was like Neil Armstrong setting his foot on the moon for the first time.

Asthamatic lungs bursting to keep pace with Anita's long strides, the poor father trudged along oblivious of the fact that his wife and Anita's mother was on the threshold of getting into a mental depression. How else could you cope up with a young daughter walking out of the house in such troubled times? Where the fairer sex were hiding in the darkest corners of houses, this one was running in the open distributing invitation cards and inviting trouble. Wave after wave of high tides, whirlwinds, earth-quakes, volcanoes, tsunami in the form of humans invaded the territory and destroyed everything in its path. Goonda (Bad) elements and vagabonds form the backbone and spine of all such catastrophes; after all this is their only work and the only time where they squeeze out their salaries and eke out a living.

There were no taxis or even rickshaws (pedal driven three wheelers) in such troubled times, so Anita kept enquiring about the way to the railway station much to the consternation of the crowd to see such a dazzling beauty walk through the streets except for the father, huffing and puffing like an engine on a steep gradient like the Darjeeling Toy train, trying to follow at a distance.

Slowly a crowd of onlookers, ruffians, peeping Toms and above all fanatics were gathering around 'the Honey' like a colony of ants. Unaware that the bee-keepers had come to pluck the honey-combs for honey, Anita kept walking in a trance, drowned in the thoughts of Neil.

Optimism and pessimism walk almost side by side. Optimists looking for the silver lining in the dark clouds and dreaming of the chocolate house that their mother told them innumerable times at the bed-side story time. A pessimist would for a fleeting second see the silver lining and his gaze would be fixed on the dark clouds signifying inherent trouble looming over the head. No evil thoughts pervaded Anita's head. She only knew she was on her way to meet her sweet-heart Neil. He would just pick her up in his muscular hands and sway her from side to side as though she was a rag doll, most precious to a child. Just hide that doll away and see the house turning topsy-turvy. Neil would squeeze Anita so tightly that she would scream "Leave me, you'll break my ribs" hoping he would never release his hold of her and he would never disappoint her for his hold would grow tighter and her crimson-red lips would turn pale with the lock of the lips-his on hers.

Anita wanted such moments never to end. Long after she would re-live those prized moments and for hours she would dive into those oceans of thought, surface out of the water drenched to the core in his love and thoughts. She was soaked in his love like a chalk in Waterman's spilt ink. The adulation of her fervour was equally matched with the tightening of his grip. His love for her would reach such a crescendo that he would want his full body to be usurped by her as you see sometimes a snake shedding its skin. He would nibble at her ears whilst she would be lost deep in his thoughts. She would even go so far as her kids playing with her father and mother. Both the grand-parents would enjoy playing 'Hide and Seek' and get so much solace from it that their life-span increased like the neck of a giraffe. Raising Anita had a lot of responsibility and lesser enjoyment whereas now it was sheer happiness with no strings attached of responsibility. Anita was just head-over-heels in love with Neil but then every lover claims that. The only way to come to the core of the truth is when the lovers separate. For some the eyes wander and for the true ones it grows fonder.

The hard breathing that she felt she suffered brought Anita back to reality from her reverie, as she strutted along the road oblivious of the multitude of people gathered to see the fun; people working in Walkers and Gazers non-existent company, Peeping Toms and way-side Romeos. It was not Germany or any of the European countries where people keep to themselves but India where anybody's business is everybody's business. Such a pokey-nose and a cohesive and close-knit society is difficult to find anywhere in the world. Indians would not be Indians if they did not know the neighbour's name, the number of children in the family, the work place, the salaries they draw, the lady he is friendly in the office, in the neighbourhood which man his wife is friendly with and if there is a grown up daughter which boy she is friendly with or she has already eloped with him etc. This is India where love reigns and when it rains it pours. Hatred has the same affinity the way love has and this was a time when undivided India was cut into two pieces—India and Pakistan and the frenzy with which it was cut was abhorrent. Throats were slit open as though broiler chicken meat was on sale.

Unawares Anita was parading all her wares and it was something everyone would love to eye, even furtively for such was her beauty that it took a colossal effort to take your eyes off her. At such a junction where a country was splitting into two which side would the vertebral column be so that it could stand straight morally and physically. Maybe another spine may grow but what about that particular time when a delicacy was served on a platter and eyes and hands found it difficult to resist the temptation. The keeper, Anita's father was flirting with the idea whether his legs would carry him further or would collapse. His chest was heaving to collect even the slightest traces of oxygen and if a doctor put his stethoscope it would sound like an army band playing the drums. Anita's father could hardly carry himself, then how could he be the good Samaritan and the good shepherd to look after his daughter. There was a retinue of gazers and for how long would these wolves stay away from their prey. At such times, the human race only turns to God for solace. Anita's father was no different. Secretly he was muttering a rosary, like Sadhus (Holy Men) do prayers on their beads, and hoping that the Almighty God with his invisible magic wand would perform a miracle for all to see and Anita would be in the clasp of Neil and everything would be fine as in fairyland.

Reality did not dawn that Neil was miles away taking long strides to diminish this distance between the two of them.

The mother of Anita even at this age, with slightly wrinkled skin, still looked an epitome of beauty. Streams of tears made furrows on her sun-tanned but ivory white skin, like a tractor would do on a fertile field. Ladies from the neighbourhood had gathered around to console her. Nothing could console her even her tongue had betrayed her. It was all parched and words would perilously linger and she found it difficult to spit it out from her hoarse throat. It seemed like Mount Vesuvius, the dormant volcano in Sicily, Italy, had become active and erupted in her throat drying and burning even her palate. Words just got burnt out and what spilled out from her mouth was a lecherous hoarse sound engulfing all the sweetness of her silken voice.

From Asaf Ali road in Daryaganj, Delhi, Neil ran and when his lungs conceded victory to nature he just slumped himself against a tree or a pillar to regain his breath. Mohammad Ali, Joe Frazier the boxers or even our wrestler, Dara Singh have their limitations to physical strength and ultimately concede to nature and God. 'God willing everything will be okay' is a refrain you hear from the commonest people to the Royals. Even the Holy books manifest 'that the spirit is willing but the flesh is weak.' In Neil's case, the spirit was more than willing and he was desperate to hold Anita and never leave her again. He was just getting mad at the very thought and the turmoil he was going through cannot be understood by any Tom, Dick and Harry except those who have been through the thick and thin of love.

Like pickle soaked in oil, Neil was soaked in that ivory doll's love, Anita. Like ice-bergs most of the mango pieces are inside the oil so was Neil's love deeper than the deepest seas.

When at last Neil reached Kashmere Gate in Delhi, the hub for buses, he was like the proverbial dog that ran and ran after the bone and when it reached the bone it was too tired to enjoy it. A fleet of buses stood in front of him. He asked for Amritsar buses but no reply came. Everyone was busy. It was most surprising in a country like India where courtesy reigns supreme. If you asked even a stranger the way to some place, chances are he would come on his motor-cycle to show you half the way. What happened today then? Partition of the country was taking place; a civil war was on. This was a time when everyone looked after their own families. Neil found two buses for Amritsar in Punjab state but where were the drivers? Trouble was brewing like hot coffee everywhere and which driver was insane to look for trouble. Every facet of life had collapsed. This was the last straw he was holding onto but the bus service had deceived him. There was no aeroplane service to the newly formed country-Pakistan and if there was one, it was not in operation for small fries like Neil. He was even ready to walk. Train services were also unreliable. With millions searching for new homes nothing was certain. Crazy things have been done in life but nothing crazier than when one is in love.

Sagging features of Anita's mother could not hide her demure looks which peeped unobtrusively from behind her wrinkles. Anyone saw her would only opine "Ooh! And Aah! and must have been a stunning beauty in her days." Anita while still in her stomach had managed to pilfer, which off-springs normally do, all her genes which were inherent in her today. The mother was aghast to see her replica going crazy and walking out of the house and the poor father trying to catch up with her who was proud as a pea-cock to have a daughter as pretty as his wife. India has changed a lot which is noticeable in the cities but not so in the villages. Much of the corruption in our country is related to gathering of this unthinkable, huge amount of dowry. Poor fathers have to pay through their nose or else their daughter is ill-treated especially by the mother-in-law who surprisingly is also a girl. The father on no account can be excused for he is very much part of the game. Life is time and time is fleeting. So let down your hair and enjoy what life has given you. Live and let live for life is very short. A child comes crying in this world and normally it continues for most of us, rich or poor. The poor for want of food cry and the rich for excess of food get obese and sickly and live on pills prescribed by the doctor. Excess of money has never made anyone happy and never will—Happiness is directly proportional to your contentment and satisfaction. A doctor will stop a ichy-rich from eating a pure ghee paratha (Indian Bread fried in oil) because of his ailing heart whereas an ordinary person will eat a brown, crisp paratha. Who is richer, you guess?

Today Anita's mother's wrinkles were heaving up and down to save the piercing beauty which was gasping for breath and quietly at logger-heads with the Almighty. She had no strength to fight with God for her own life but in her speechless quiet way she could beseech the CREATOR to pave her daughter's way to happiness. Parents can wish for nothing better.

Atleast twenty eyes of the neighbourhood were keeping around the clock vigil on her condition even in those God-forsaken days of a civil war. One gazelle shaped, dark brown eyes of one lady were moist who was trying to give as much comfort to Anita's mother as she could. One pair of piercing eyes just sat minding everyone's business. One pair of eyes couldn't face reality and just sat with eyes closed. Inside her eyes, what volcano erupted nobody knew nor cared. One lady sat staring into eternity with rivulets of tears down her cheeks. One just wanted the mother's other leg also to go into the grave so that death came easily and peacefully. It did. She closed her eyes and never opened again—she had gone to the next world. The words on a last pilgrimage bus kept staring and penetrating with a piercing thud 'Death is the wish of some, relief of many and the end of all'.

Anita's father had left a crying wife at home and did not know that he would ever need a handkerchief to wipe her tears again, but then no thoughts endeared him into thinking about her. On the silver screen of his mind was engraved in big letters 'Anita' and he was gasping for breath following his daughter.

The armour of calm that Neil wore all his life was slowly rusting. The sheen had withered and in its place a ruthlessness had walked in, seizing him by his shoulders and shaking him like a rag-doll in a dog's mouth to wake him from his slumber of thoughts and put them in alphabetical order to straighten out his plan of action to reach his ultimate destination, his love, Anita.

Before this, his thoughts had been roaming far and wide. Why people wanted to divide one land into different countries? Why India was knifed into two through the hearts of the people which bled and suffered. Just a handful of opulent people with borrowed muscles and no conscience are at the threshold of such perverse activities. They are power-thirsty and with power comes the Goddess of crisp, tantalizing green notes, money. The world gets crazy counting a plethora of soiled and crisp paper currency that they accumulate over the years.

It is really intoxicating and people get drunk in its midst and forget they are humans and behave more like robots drooling from their mouths only to take revenge and vent their ire on the opposite party.

The rays of thought going far and wide, all emanated from only one source, Anita. As Neil walked in his deep thoughts, he wondered why the Pacific Ocean came in the middle to separate North America from Asia and South America from Australia. Did the waves at low tide and high tide roar with laughter to see the land touching each other and then receding? Did the Atlantic Ocean take pride in keeping away the affinity of the east side of Americas with the west side of the great continent of

Africa and that of Europe? Where the Indian Ocean or the Bay of Bengal failed to cover the idiosyncrasies of India, man's greed and jealousy stepped in to divide the country into two—India and Pakistan. How wonderful it would have been when the Earth's Land and water (as it was millions of years ago) formed different huge masses of land and water when our Earth was called PANGAEA.

Neil's thoughts clouded his vision when something hard struck him with speed and force. It was a motor-cycle with a mad man speeding to get away to someone near and dear. The mad man did not realize that the one he lacerated would recuperate without a doctor and was he on his way to meet and ignite his love? Would he ever dine with his lady-love or just pine for her? Where do such thoughts ever enter a stranger's gray matter otherwise wouldn't the world be a lovely place to live in?

Neil was picked up by the pulsating, unwieldily crowd that created quite a pandemonium and it grew faster than weeds. Acceding to the fact that he may have broken a rib or so, Neil got up, fell, got up again and gyrated his way out of the crowd. You think Neil walked, well he nearly trotted like a horse and would have galloped had all the harness inside his body been fine. The thought of Anita was gnawing him like a rat a piece of bread. With every step, the agonizing pain slowed him down but the smiling, inviting face of Anita made him keep his momentum. He lunged forward to get into her arms but each time he only licked the dust. It was plain hallucination. 'Dust thou art and into dust returneth' he would recall. So this dust walks and talks for almost 60 to 80 years and then reclines in the grave or burnt till it is dust and Tom, Dick and Harry no more.

Dark clouds of urchins had already formed a silhouette in the horizon but that Neil had his head on his shoulders (as though Ricky has his head on his arm—Ha, ha silly joke, did you say? Give a constipated laugh and relieve your stress) was the silver lining at the edges of the clouds.

Neil knitted warm and cozy sweaters with words that fitted anyone comfortably and swerved them in the direction of the crowd that favoured him. No untoward incident took place and he was miles away from the unsavoury crowd and harm—so be it—Amen.

What's in a Name

How did Anita living in Germany for so long know about Wagah or the Attari border separating the newly found country, Pakistan from India. The scent of love pervades everywhere and this was a mountain of a cancerous tumour coming in between their satin-smooth lives. She did not shudder for a moment that she could be on the wrong track. Intuition told her she was in the right direction; she would stop momentarily to ask her wayside admirers and her sixth sense cajoling and promising her the verdure of Adam and Eve's garden.

Reeking with such entwined tendrils of thought she left her father far behind in this race. Masquerading as her well-wishers, the scum of the city were gathering like a colony of ants for sugar. Their eyes just bulged out as though increasing the area of their eyes would soak in more of her devastating beauty. Their mouths drooled and their hands itched to touch the 'Touch-me-Not'. They had a burning desire to touch but did not gather enough guts to even go close. Dainty steps of Anita kept her steady gait and you would believe she was out of harm's way. They followed her like a toddler a mother.

Suddenly out of the blues there was a shriek of 'Help, help' when around ten muscular men were chasing a man in blue clothes. One shot on the head with a bamboo stick made a fountain of red hot blood ooze out. "Why do you want to kill me"? "Because you are an infidel and do not belong to our true religion" and with that the swishing of a sword could be heard followed by the gushing of thick, red blood from his chest and then the thud of his body falling on the ground. It was a scene of a shikari (hunter) with the hounds after a hare. My pen is refusing to move forward after such an orgy. My eyes are moist and a translucent curtain has fallen on them that I cannot find and read in the Bible, The Quran or The Bhagwad Gita where it says you have to kill for your religion. No religion teaches us to even hurt anyone, leave alone kill. All religions would boil down to one word—'LOVE', then why all this mayhem. This certainly then is the work of some unscrupulous persons. Humans and mankind beware or it may become too late—The world stands on the brink of disaster. The word 'malice' does not stand the scrutiny of any civilized society.

When such heinous crimes are committed, the eyes can see but cannot perceive, the brain is blocked and all the gray matter in the brain must be taking on an evil hue or gone on a vacation. The left hand does not know what atrocity the right hand is witness to. Excuses to kill you may find many but a thumping victory for mankind lies in its total abstinence. Take it or Fake it.

With a boasting glee, after the killing, these evil bulls turn their roving eyes to reconnoitre the fastest trail to the baffling beauty. Such flawless, pretty girls had only to be touched and caressed and no harm should ever befall them. Their parched lips waiting to pine and dine on hers. Their itchy hands were eagerly awaiting to grasp handfuls of her silky-smooth flesh.

With curtains of religion drawn, these ruffians manouevre to come as close as they could to her. "Why do you harass her?" they shout in their most vulgar, debase and guttural voices for their head is a store-house of filthy abuses. The crowd bellows "She ain't one of us but from across the border". Trying to touch her which is their aim "What's your name"? When Anita does not heed to their queries they ferociously repeat the question. She demurely replies "Anita". Anita finding herself in such a perplex situation tries to pacify them that she is not who they are looking for is greeted with boos, laughter and ridicule.

"What's in a name"? I remember all the debating societies feverishly fighting to put their point in. Today what I'm witnessing will leave no doubt in anyone's mind. A name can spell death or life. It is always the common man on the road, at the behest of some fanatic goons and musclemen who brings miseries to himself and inflicts miseries on others. Now what was their business to torture a young girl who was on her way to meet her lover and decidedly future husband. She was so imbrued and inundated in his love that she could not think of anything except him. Then where lay the fault that she was trespassing somebody's private property? Who were these people to pass judgements of death? Self appointed judges who use Religion as their shields to kill someone. A civil war was on which should not even have taken root. You go your way, I go mine. Where does blood-shed come in the picture? Instigators are always there who do all the mischief and then vanish from the scene. The only thing that can rescue the common man is education which will reveal the shrewdness with which these manipulating people make the common man a scape-goat. He just ushers to the whims and fancies of his masters. I have gone miles away from the story to make people aware of the truth but they will see but not perceive; their ear-drums will burst but no guile of their masters they will notice. Till they are bereft of education and of free thinking, they will remain slaves. All the A, B, C, D—are in disarray—they have to sort them out to make sense.

"You said your name is Anita" shouted another hungry eyed Joe ready to pounce on her. "Yes, yes I'm Anita. Anita comes from the East and the West with a slight difference in pronunciation. Even my husband to be, who I'm going to meet is Neil. He comes from the same denomination as I am and yet there is another name with the same pronunciation but different spellings—"NEEL", explained Anita in her placid and yet lilting, demure but shaky voice. All the explanation went over their blocked heads. Their hands were already red in blood from the killing and now blood was rising in their eyes too. They had just killed a man and it would be fun killing a woman, a lady at that, who could very well go for a memsahib with attributes starting from her Venus' face to a lovely, long drawn neck that a Kohinoor diamond would feel proud to adorn. The attributes of her pretty face would leave any man's gaze frozen. Seeing her further would make him weak and helpless, such sensuous beauties lived only in dreams.

These creatures of the dust, these earth-worms, these parasites wanted to touch and crawl on her luscious body. In all her innocence how could she avert such hyenas, ready to pounce on her any moment.

The Price of Partition

A truck laden with belongings and a family of husband and wife with two children and an old, shriveled mother to let him travel with them as they were fleeing from India to Pakistan. Why a family with a young wife would allow a total stranger, a very young man, to travel along looks shrouded in mystery. Perhaps his coming along would save the family from bad elements and vagabonds and road-side romeos. His name Neil was synonymous with the other name Neel. Later when they had become quite familiar with each other, Neil told her all about his love for Anita and he was going to Lahore to meet her. She was his everything. The husband's gaze was constantly on the hard, stern look of the road which pleads with every driver to go slow as it rocks the vehicle in it's arms like a mother; sometimes spanking it by breaking the axle as it goes on the bumps and speed-breakers with uncontrollable and break-neck speeds. At 45kilometres per hour, the road like a mother would entice the vehicle with the best average that all, especially Indians, look for in a car. At 70-80 kilometres per hour it smothers it with kisses but above 100 kilometres per hour it takes it as a wayward child and unable to hold it firmly in it's grasp. Oblivious to Neil, whose pupils of the eyes dilated for just a glimpse of Anita, there were road-side shows going on inspite of a civil war being on. Early in the morning these perennial actors would drown their sorrows in a 'Patiala Peg' or a pint of liquor and their antics with their legs and hands would put in the shade all the clowns and jokers. My dear boys and girls, big and small, life is so precious that man is ready to do anything to save it from harm's way unless respect, love and honour come in for which he can die. Fortunately the two children were too small or so Neil felt but if they said 'Ammi' instead of 'mummy' or 'Amma' their game would be up and they would never reach their destination, Pakistan. Even if the children uttered 'Abba' instead of 'Daddy 'or 'Pitaji' they would mercilessly be slaughtered and there would be no dusk or dawn for them anymore. My dear friends who are laboriously turning the sheaves of this novel put yourself in the situation and plight of the characters and you will learn to enjoy life instead of dragging it day after day. Life is so beautiful, only learn to enjoy it.

One person kills and their whole community has to pay with their lives. Justice indeed in the name of religion. Shards of glass must have pierced their near and dear ones to ogle out a portrait of hatred, one religion against another. When will people wake up from their ignorance or is Religion purposely used as a fishing hook to catch the fish the master's fancy?

India and Pakistan saw the biggest exodus of rivulets of refugees from one country to the other.

On the ground the lines of refugees looked like a convoy of army trucks on the move. From a Helicopter it looked like a colony of ants, minus their whispers to each other, in search of a new home with harrowing tales that one could not hear without eyes getting moist and blurred. Wave after wave of people in Ox-driven carts, horse drawn tongas, trucks or the most reliable transport of all, slow but sure, their two feet entwined like branches of trees.

Chaos reigned both the countries and ruffians had a hey-day extorting valuables from unsuspecting ladies and weak men. People were carrying all the jewelry and cash they had amassed over the years on their person and if they fell in these musclemen's clutches, paranoid with fear of their lives they would hand over all their life's earnings. Overnight these goons and beggars had an esquire written in front of their names on the name-plate for they were now millionaires.

Neil and company, inspite of all the pandemonium were lucky to squeeze through the impenetrable traffic on the road, slow but sure. Black clouds with a silver lining would sprout in the sky and vanish with the same alacrity bringing relief and cheer and despair simultaneously especially those who believed in myths of the old wives tales. If a black cat crossed the road their destination was blurred.

Rumours would filter and sometimes, though seldom, the truth would pervade like lightening that so many men, women and children were slaughtered on the other side of the fence. Repercussions would follow and the unlucky ones who came in this stride would be put to the sword.

Neil and his protégées got caught in such a quagmire. The vengeance seekers looked at Neil, admired him and just let him pass along with his people. 'There's many a slip between the cup and the lip' is a saying which fits like a penny in a slot in this case. One minute there was every likelihood of all getting shot dead but because of Neil all were saved. They couldn't have been more grateful to Neil. As the wheels of the truck started rolling "Ammi Jaan (Mum), why are these people stopping our truck"? shouted the big child to his mother in his screechy voice while the mother tried to put a lid on his mouth with the palms of her hand but the truth was already in the air. Seething with disgust, the angry crowd jumped onto the truck while it sped on. Someone put a spanner or an iron rod in one of the wheels and the truck came to a screeching, grinding halt. Fire-works flew out due to the friction of the rod and the wheel but compared to the heat of the hatred in every eye it was Luke-warm. The two children were just pulled out from the shielding arms of the father and mother and thrown out of the truck like live chickens from one cage to another. There was bewilderment, consternation and fear in the eyes of the children. What was going behind the depths of the oceans of the eyes was entirely inexplicable. The face and eyes are covered so that the pleadings and entreaties of the prisoner does not falter the hang-man from putting the noose. In front of the dazed eyes of the parents the two children were crushed to death like children crush ants under their shoes. The frail grand-mother just jumped behind the children and died on the spot. The crowd was rejoicing. Surely man has got animal blood in him, how else would he take pride in such beastly killings. A beast kills to fill his stomach, what cravings does a man have to fill?

From nowhere a barber's razor appeared in the husband's hand. The wife pushed her head back to show a white, gazzelle's taut neck. The hand did not quiver nor showed signs of remorse when the husband with one swipe of the razor slit the wife's neck while the red blood spluttered out in protest. To save his wife's honour the husband had to kill her. I leave it to the reader's imagination what all the unruly mob of unscrupulous goons would have done to her, surely nothing very pleasing. In any war, women have suffered the worst agonies.

The husband was made to run while the crowd ran behind him, on top of him with shoe kicks. They wanted to kill him but not before he suffered. He was hit, bruised with hands, sticks till he turned to pulp. Not satisfied some even tried to peel off his skin with the help of a blade and when they found no resistance coming from his side the sword did the last rites of extremunction to send him to his logical end. The body lay quivering not with fright but with no blood flowing in the arteries and veins, for everything was over. He was dead.

Neil was stunned to see five lively, harmless people killed so easily. Man was really weak, so he found today. The dead bodies lay in awkward positions. Some of the crowd melted to gather the remains of the dead to show their last respects and put them in a presentable position. He found man very illogical and funny. First kill and then show your respects to the dead. "Love me when I'm alive, death will not make any difference how you treat me", he thought.

The crowd had finished with the dead, now they turned their attention to the one alive, Neil. Ruffians and villains had taken five lives, will religion act as a shield or an arrow for the sixth. The deep rooted trees stood at the sides of the road swaying with the gentle breeze as though acknowledging the sufferings of the human race and trying to fan their sorrows away without success. The

High and Mighty, Almighty, it seemed, had not woken up from HIS slumber. When the swish of His wand was enough to alleviate the miseries of the human flesh and bones that creaked as though age was the biggest weight to carry for the 'Race' of the humans from birth till the spirit says adieu to the beautifully sculpted body and it goes limp. Lords and kings came, ruled and then gifted their bodies to the good earth in their everlasting sleep. So did my dad and so will I, then why this arrogance when ultimately we'll be maimed. The Petunias in the garden turned their heads like bugles welcoming the tired out new country seekers. The Holly-Hocks grew taller to peek into the affairs of the new arrivals. The Sweet-Peas climbed higher using their tendrils for support to spread their lovely inviting fragrance. The Snap-Dragons (or the Dog Flower as we called in childhood) were the only flowers ready to snap at the flow of strangers but their mouths were shut for there were no boys to press the necks for the mouths to open. The grass kept it's silken back ready to caress the tired out backs of strangers to soothe them. The only one ready to maim and cripple the starved people was man himself. What arrogance with a perishable body. Just think man, just think! But we are myopic and short-sighted to think so far.

Many stood awe-struck with Neil's staggering stature, but the muscular loafers among them with tongues long enough to beat a giraffe had the audacity and nerve to call him a trespasser for they wanted to show-off with their muscles. This was a lovely time to test them. Neil tried to shout louder that he was not the one they wanted but his lone voice was drowned in the quagmire of filth emanating from the filthy, venomous tongues of the blood curdling crowd. The vagabonds asked him to prove his faith and he said the Lord's prayer to prove his antecedents. He closed his eyes and very fervently beseeched God to save him from this calamity and have, atleast, a last look for the one he pined for, Anita.

"Our Father, Who art in Heaven, Hallowed be Thy Name, Thy Kingdom come—" and the crowd was aghast that the orgy they had planned had altered and faltered. The veneer Neil wore on his handsome face was indeed real, with tendrils of his faith sunk deep into him, caressing and bringing solace to these masquerading logger-heads.

The crowd came like a huge, colossal tsunami and receded like a whimpering puppy setting the prisoner free.

Neil jumped on to the vacant driver's seat of the truck. The key was in its place but the engine was not purring. He turned the key and the ignition responded instantly. He stepped on the accelerator, the truck sprang like a tiger. There was a 'thud' noise of the collision of the truck and a dog which had jumped up from its sleep underneath the truck and now was taking eternal sleep. What a way for a dog to die? Maybe it had a dog's death. Man doesn't care for a man's death then what is a dog? Not a furrow of his fore-head twitches, what is man made up of? Indeed man's disaster lies in his own hands. He is more volatile than an Atom Bomb. An atom bomb needs a command from a man to fire and cause disaster. He does not need a detonator to ignite—carry on, my dear boys! Carry on.

Neil drove at break-neck speed smothering not with kisses, but with the brutality and force of the truck causing anything in its path to disintegrate. It was now an empty truck for everything that was in it had been taken away by the looting, pilfering crowd. Overnight rags to riches story was enacted in reality. How many houses had been washed away in the ocean of wrath of the people. People who had never held gold in the palms of their hands were holding gold and diamonds in their tight fists without knowing they had turned millionaires. The truck sped on. Music as usual flowed from the tyres and the road but there was something ominous and sinister in it's screeching tune as people gather from the hooting of an owl

In those days if the G.P.S. had arrived which today science has made big leaps and strides to conquer, Neil would have reached Anita's house with ease. He had to repeatedly stop or slow down to make queries where to turn and which road to take for the Wagah Border for

Lahore. Some people answered him hurriedly as though scared, some menacingly but may have been timid as a hare from inside. A civil war was on and people were going through an agonizing time where friends and foes could not be trusted. All lived in trepidation and fear of getting butchered. Much to the consternation of Neil, he had come into Lahore and into Anita's territory. His heart was thumping and pumping at an unusual rate. He could visualize Anita with open arms on the doorway to clasp him for eternity, never to leave again. Neil was talking to himself while a halo of happiness and butterflies in his stomach surrounded his beaming face. He felt so close and yet so far. When he had almost reached his destination, he felt the roads had elongated with the heat of the Sun. The road did welcome him with an elongated kiss to his tyres and the 'Black Beauty' (the road) welcomed a fair and handsome face to Anita's door. Just like the north and south poles of two magnets attract each other black and white also have an affinity for each other. He saw some ladies wailing, some sitting quietly next to an ice-cold body. It was Anita's mother, somebody whispered in a drooping voice and her father had gone towards the railway station. Neil darted out like a mad arrow out of the string of the bow. The crowd behind Anita cried hoarse with eerie noises. They were more into fun following a lady, a ravishingly beautiful lady. They would never, ever get a chance to come close, leave alone touch her with their leathery, wart infested hands.

A plethora of agonizing moments lay at her feet, only God's miracle would stop the contagious hooting and cajole these people from pining to dine on her. The ooh! Ah! Wow! was heaving with excitement as was the bosom of her chest with fright and trepidation. Her father, it looked, had turned into a statue of stone. The usual question arose like smoke from a chimney of a brick kiln. "What is your name"? they barked. "Anita" she said demurely. "Ah, ha! she is not of our faith, kill her, kill her". She tried to pacify them that Anita was a name common in both East and Western countries. What's in a name was evident today. A name could mean life or death. Even her boy-friend who she wanted to meet and marry had the same pronunciation 'NEEL' and 'NEIL'. She was getting desperate as she took long strides to get out of harm's way. The more she tried, the closer they got. What had saved Neil, they asked her too. She had become so confused with the thronging crowd that she could not utter beyond "OUR FATHER, OUR FATHER, OUR FATHER" She poured out the dictionary, but all the A, B, C—were in disarray. She tried sorting it out but the LORD's PRAYER could not be connected. She tried to explain but her pleas were all in vain. "Liar, Liar" rant the air.

From a distance a vehicle could be seen rushing. As it came closer it turned out to be a truck and Neil on the driver's seat. He was soon pulled out and queries made.

In the midst of the crowd, Neil's eyes fell on Anita. He shouted "ANITA "and ran towards her. Their eyes met with relief. In the stampede that followed one fanatic drew out his sword and with one swipe cut off Anita's head which landed into the running Neil's hands.

Neil just sank to the ground on his knees with Anita's head in his lap and her eyes looking into his eyes with love.

"Enough, enough of your nonsense, send him also to his girl" someone shouted from the crowd.

They pushed and pulled him, but he was stiff. He was dead from the shock of Anita's head in his arms.